Prothalamium

A CYCLE OF

A NOVEL BY PHILIP TOYNBEE

Prothalamium

THE HOLY GRAAL

GREENWOOD PRESS, PUBLISHERS
WESTPORT, CONNECTICUT

Notation of the Book Everything which appears in italics is overheard by the narrator, but said neither by him nor to him.

The pages are numbered both according to the period and events described (by the number itself), and according to the narrator (by the letter attached to the number). Thus page A7 covers the same period as pages B7, C7 and so on, but each is the experience of a different person. A narrator always begins at the point of his entry into the room, and concludes at his departure from it. Thus narrator F's account opens on a page marked F6 (and not F1) because it is not until time-unit 6 that she enters the room. Thus narrator B's account is numbered from B1 to B12, because he is present throughout the whole twelve pages covered by the book.

The following plan should make the notation clear:

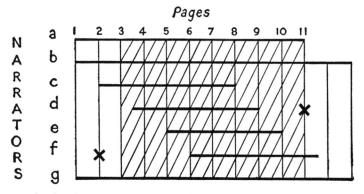

The book progresses along the horizontal lines from left to right and downwards, as in reading. Pages A1 to A10 are followed by pages B1 to B12, followed by pages C2 to C7, and so on. The faint vertical lines represent simultaneous moments of time. There is no page F2 (point crossed above) because narrator F is not yet in the room at page 2. Similarly there is no page D11 because narrator D has left the room by time-unit 11. The meaning of the shaded portion should become apparent in the course of the book.

Prothalamium

A1   **Max Ford** In joy I claim Mrs. Goodman: I knew
her instantly for my special hostess, and knew myself her
chosen guest. "Tom, I claim Mrs. Goodman." Yet I have
only murmured it, hummed it to a summer tune; and Tom
is deaf. In the nursery he would grant this sickly elder
brother a quota of such claims, confined to my sharpest
needs, my most implacable desires. And by those old prece-
dents he'll surely grant me this; for why should he covet the
warm nest that's Mrs. Goodman, or long, as I do, to be an
egg in it? Tom, I claim her.

Now the larks over Lemnos ream out the frowning memory of our first arrival, and I can recall it to forget it. There
was some pity in her smile, welcoming me to that one high
Jacobean chair. Down I sat, in trust, in confidence, to
CRASH, the carved legs splaying backwards from the seat. It
was Tom, dear brother in his dearest, most familiar role,
who picked up the chair, banged it twice with his oarsman's
fist, sat squarely and securely down on it himself.

And now the room's all blue and gold. The wild vine
climbs through the sunny corner window, and writhes at the
fluted lamp-stand. On the mantelpiece a dried, spiny urchin
saltens the air. Boulders tumble under the cypresses and
there, bone-white and dry above us, is the Parthenon. All
the scents and ghosts of the south are in this room, dry gold
of my Aegean, the lemon and the lizard; the encrusted bed
of the sea, clear as my hand through forty feet of lucent
water. And here too is the rainless fertility of Syrian gardens, beside the bloody rivers of Adonis.

By my hostess sits Daisy's blooming brother, damp black
curls and heavy lashes, young enough to be the lady's son.
How silently he blooms, this Noel Tillett; with what assurance! But come now, Max, my foolish dear, you must feel no
antipathy, for he's NOT her son. Graciously, graciously he
too will recognize your claim, and dance, brown-eyed, full-
lipped, the ceremony of your adoption in the olive grove.
Only in the bloom of his skin is he his sister's brother, his   14

white and pink and golden sister, your love. Oh, when, when, when will she come?

"Thank you, Mrs. Goodman. Let me see . . ."

With just that same tender air of knowing, she offers us a plate of coffee-coated biscuits, on each a white sugar animal embossed. For its crouched legs and streaming ears, for its gentle but mistrustful eye, I choose the hare; Tom, for his own bold reasons, the bull. What Tillett chose I couldn't see, but Mrs. Goodman laughs with curious pleasure at his choice. Laugh for me, Mrs. Goodman, and see with those cradling eyes the delicacy bedded in my indelicate face. And in return I'll proclaim you the poetess of vineyards, autumnal beekeeper and guardian of the field-mouse. Under the canopy of grape and vine-leaf I'll lay my head on your aproned lap, and listen to your old stories of the vineyard.

A2 And is it you, at last, my girl of the golden legs, girl of the canteloupe and Enna's flowers? Yes, again within my sight and hearing, within my touch, image of the maiden loved when I was ten, when I was twenty-two, when I was thirty. And I shall be all those loving ages again to love her now. In Syracuse and on the shore at Hamamet, girl of the Improvident Sea, who sang to the fishermen at sunset. Richly incarnate she stands before the hostess, my Daisy Tillett, my girl of the sea, my girl of the sun.

Mrs. Goodman smiles above the silver kettle and motions to a chair. Now I'd have the poetess adopt the maid, teach her to grow from this perfection of youth to just such a bosomed glow of middle-age. Be mentor, my Mrs. Goodman, to my Daisy.

"Well, Tom, are you glad you came?"

Thus, turning to my brother beside me, I've tried to stir this dumb happiness to expression. For such dreams, I know, must be given the dull compelling reality of words; or they are lost, and doubted for ever afterwards.

But Tom is deaf again, his oyster-opening eyes fixed stubbornly on Daisy's brother, all his stern attention levelled like a gun. *"I feel certain, Tillett,"* he says, *"that I've seen you somewhere before."* So I must think that Tom has felt it too, the merciless flux of all that's left unspoken. But the boy smiles lightly and answers that he's travelled a good deal; no more; not snubbing Tom, but halting the interrogation there. An enigmatic boy! Well his enigma's nothing to the mystery which shines about us all. For who in all this northern city would believe that we could be so near them, yet a season and a meridian away. Who'd think that so much southern joy could live in Coburg Square, behind these foggy Georgian walls.

Indeed my joy's so sure that now, when Daisy's smile flies like a bird at me across the table, I feel it no special act of grace, but rather a token of a love which has no need of any token. I'd live in a southern garden with them both, grafting   *16* this tendril of wild vine to the old vintage stem of Mrs. Goodman. You, Tom, with your stern back and restless face, shall work among the olives, ride over the mountain for our bread, catch crayfish off the harbour. And Noel shall be a sea-blown statue on the terrace, forever young, preserving his enigma until the terrace falls. How full a contrast that would be to Lilly. Oh, no, no, no, Max, be forgetful now, and raise your pinions to the sun. Be Icarus, be Phaeton and Bellerophon, but live for ever at the topmost moment.

Thank you, Mrs. Goodman. *"Thank you, Mrs. Goodman,"* echoes Daisy Tillett, taking HER biscuit from the proffered plate. Now, give me NOW your smile. It's true that I'd imagined I could do without it, but now I confess that something of Lilly weighs me down. Ah, let me stay near the sun! Daisy, let me stay there! But down and down now, as the teacup falls from Mrs. Goodman's hand.

A3   Within my head, behind my eyes, a face describes the dial
of a clock, now revolving slower, now pausing at five to
midday to swing down and round and up again to five past
midnight; now a pendulum from nine to three; at last hangs
quivering at six o'clock. Oh, I know you, Mrs. Goodman, my
old bitch, whore and familiar; harlot of the afternoon in
Islington, of the night in Genoa and the night at Colwyn
Bay. Damp from the last client, your bust-bodice is split by
giant udders, thighs are swollen to bounce on, and a wooded
hell's cut deep for my concealment. Cthonic lady of the
back streets, under your German mountain, I'll sin for a
thousand years, my armour rusting.

Yes, there she bends her quivering torso to lift the shards,
piling them together on the unbroken saucer. Trembling
above her stands the boy, no less transformed, grey as the
dead, and with mildew on his hair. Now she hands him the
broken teacup: he bows a little, accepts it like a eucharist on
open palms, turns and stumbles to the door. Goodbye to
unregretted youth.

A wind blows freezing from the opened door, and Daisy
shrinks and shivers. Is there blood in the wind?

Yet it seems that our little circle is not to be reduced.
Who's this grey hobbler at the door, crouched on a stick,
his black clothes aglow with the mossy sheen of age? And
another follows, hobbling in ugly mimicry of the first. This
follower is as bald as Ossa, his face crunched up to imitate
the deeply wizened face of the old man. (Why, what a
pageant my harlot has prepared for me!) Nobody will help
the old creature to his chair. The bald one straightens his
back, smoothes out his gross bright cheeks, sits uninvited
on the chair between Tom and Daisy. Meanwhile Frau
Goodman coarsely gestures the other to the chair left vacant
beside her by poor departed Tillett; and down he creaks,
grimacing as his cracked buttocks meet the uncushioned
seat. I smell the decay of woods in winter.

Winter is running round this drawing-room, and from the   *18*

planes outside the window, green leaves are falling like a **A3**
snowstorm. Now by summoning all the strength of my eyes
I can read the titles of the largest books against the western
wall there. The *Iliad*, I see, and Shakespeare; Milton,
Goethe, the Vedantas. Now be at my side, you wise and
great and inexplicably prolific: save me from the terrors of
this hollow mountain; exorcise my fears with knowledge.
See how deep the sun has fallen into those rocks and trees
of Paul Cezanne! You too, you old embittered countryman
with dragon's eyes, come to my side and show me all the
immanent glory of the visible world.

But why should I, knowing so well that understanding
comes only from sympathy, withhold my sympathy from
these strange visitors? Why should I submit to this first
nursery impulse of hostility and fear? Old man—old PRIEST,
I see, from the grey dog-collar under your scrawny neck—
old priest, have you reached the rainbow waters of that
harbour where I long to be?

A4 Have you known the parti-coloured island where everything and its opposite is true; where every casual sequence of words proclaims another and a certain truth, as surely as every disarrangement of a kaleidoscope constructs another pattern? Do your dark eyes, Father Morton, hold the wide vision of mutilated Father Origen, old comfort of my sleepless nights, the Blessed and the Wise?

Now the harlot's livid eyes interrogate me, demanding the monstrous answer to some monstrous question; eyes of Medusa which turn the beholder not to stone but water.

"Stir up the fire, Charley. My old bones . . ."

He shakes his bones together as he says it.

"Old syphilitic bones!"

With this snort of hell's malice bald-head Charley rises to poke the fire. *"Bugger!"* he shouts above the clatter of falling embers; and then he laughs. Out of the confusion, the cries and the craning of necks, Tom jumps up with all his marvellous authority, strides to the hearth and gathers the fallen embers on a shovel. Then, brushing his surgical hands together, he reassures the company, resumes his trusty throne.

But now Daisy's eyes, fleetingly on mine, are full of grief, reproach and disappointment. For what? Oh, doubtless for my failure to forestall Tom in his bold action. But you must know, my love, that I am a hero of a different order. Danger might find me calm, but never active or resourceful. I was never the conqueror of fire, never the oarsman or the mountaineer. I have no weapons, dearest, but sympathy and knowledge: with them I've been the harrower of hells within, the stormer of my own crystal battlements. Why do you stare at my Judas brother, my Cain, who never needed you nor anyone? It's Max you should be saving with those eyes from the acrid compulsion of the harlot, for her questioning odours fill all this winter wilderness.

"The answer is Man!"

There! She has it. Away to the abyss, swollen sphynx of the street-corner and the brothel! Man is the answer, three-legged and in torment, seeking everywhere your black caves to hide his third leg in. Suppose I were to address them now, and say: "You with all your arduous achievements, what do you know of the land which Plato and Plotinus saw! What do you know of that antique wisdom of the south where truth falls with the sunlight and beauty burns over the clear sea! But I, the manic and the failure, I shall find it. I shall see God where you see only the night and a few candle-flames."

Fatal pride! Silly dream! Tom is no Cain, but simply a stronger and a more virtuous man than I.

"Don't touch her, Charley!"

What a whipcrack prohibition from so old a man! But what is he forbidden to touch, and why?

A5   A child, a little boy, pokes his red topknot round the opening door, then draws it sharply back again. "Come in, Billy," shouts Charley, a roaring ogre now—and the child cautiously reveals his whole untidy body. Squinting, spectacled and dirty, he's just such an uncouth waif as I was, nearly forty years ago. Dragging his reluctant booted feet, he circles the table, to sit, alas, beside ME. And what sharp far-off memories stir from this sour smell of urine and unwashed flesh—mattress and linoleum and a push-chair in the gardens, nanny's starch and the nightlight by my bed.

Poor boy, I'll try. . . . What, you rogue! You barbarous boy! You'd kick me! Oh, what to do, what to do, what to do to prove my peace and wisdom? Yes, boy, probe beyond my hidden legs and kick (thank God) my stalwart brother! Now what-to-do's no longer mine to answer, and Tom has never asked himself the question. See him rise again in all his punitive majesty, pass formidably behind my chair to box—one, two! the horrid creature's ears. Brave Tom; but oh, block tight MY ears against the infant screech of pain and anger.

No, my love, no! Drag your captive eyes away! He's blind and deaf, the old fierce enemy of our inheritance. No, my love, no! This tenacious sawbones was never the man to fondle you. Shall I tell you the nickname which was given him at school? How you'll laugh!

But have I lost you then?

What's left is never more than these; a broken civility, a feeble, forced curiosity. Politely and without one visible flicker of despair, I lean across the table and address the bald-head opposite. "I'm afraid I didn't quite catch your name."

"Charley Parsley is my stage name, but in private Charley Morton. Your poodle, Mr. Ford."

"Then Father Morton . . . ?"

"Is my most incarnate father. But you wouldn't blame him, would you, man of the world as I know you to be, for   22 the errors of his callow novitiate? He's old now, and under the weather, but he's a great man, Mr. Ford, though I say it."

"Well, yes, I can believe it."

"And can you believe something else, Mr. Ford. Mrs. Goodman—come a little closer—used to be a prostitute in Colwyn Bay. Twenty years from the squire to the pox."

Why should I listen when I know it all? After sin comes the night of guilt, the sunrise of repentance; and with repentance comes such a revival of the spirit that by noon we're fit to sin again. I know it all. ". . . Oh, you'll appreciate the Governor. When he's free I'll have you meet him."

For no, certainly he's not free now, but leans towards Daisy with passionate, persuasive gestures. What is it that he mutters in her ear? *"Your love will give him something far more precious than strength."* Oh, dear old man, my dearest advocate and friend. For you she'll love me even now.

A6   You're very welcome, lady of the waning moon. Another
player: another act. Her eyes are large and muddy, flaked
with gold in the pupils; her greying hair is gathered in a
low-slung bun. She walks precisely to the last empty chair
and sits abruptly down there, crying out with all her move-
ments that the company disgusts her. And an old pendulous
retriever has followed her in, his sagging jowl an inch from
the carpet.

Those eyes, that vertical remorseless chest, they evoke
some memory, some far-off trembling alarm. Who?

But oh, it WAS, it WAS a rare felicity, the time of Daisy's
first arrival, the distant salt-sea time before the boy's dis-
missal. Brief minutes of my innocence, before the Fall.

The dog has left pads of dirt across the carpet, and Tom
is already and unbidden at work with the shovel. I'd never
deny that he deserves whatever strange reward he's seeking.
From behind a raised teacup Miss Black addresses Daisy:
"I think I USED *to see you at St. Aloysius." "Yes, I used to go
there before the changes."* Now this I shall enjoy, an ecclesi-
astical dispute between the ladies;—and therefore Charley
chooses the moment to embroil me with his father. "I've
read your work with the greatest interest, Mr. Ford." Oh,
but he's a sweet and courteous old man, my dear friend.
Come, father, let's plant a garden of courtesy at this barbaric
table, leaning thus to each other and disregarding all the
militant thundering around us. "It's delightful to hear you
say so, Father Morton."

"Your version of the Hymn of the Soul is most beautiful,
most moving. May one assume that you yourself are in
Egypt, so to speak, seeking the Pearl?"

"Alas, too often forgetting my mission." (How melodiously
he laughs; and his voice is like a college lawn.)

"Do you not sometimes suspect, Mr. Ford, that those who
find the Pearl are not the best of us. The full man, the man
of thought and feeling, cannot but be attentive to the many
and beautiful distractions on his path. Straitness of purpose   24

is not a virtue which I have ever been able to esteem very highly. It has no use, you see, for the harrowing joys of human love. It allows no time for the contemplation of religious truth. Christian was so pugnacious in his barbarous progress! Why did it never occur to him that Giant Despair could have been turned into an ally, had he been treated with a proper respect?"

"Yet the Pearl" (how am I to explain!) "the Pearl is surely ALL knowledge and ALL love. It's a symbol which embraces all distractions too, all pain and pleasure, all good and evil."

"Then I fear your pearl is an hallucination, Mr. Ford. It is a symbol of impossibility. Life is conflict and contradiction, and to believe in some ultimate reconciliation is the sheerest mumbo-jumbo. It is possible, of course, to pursue some single ambition, and to neglect or deride everything which conflicts with it. But how pitiably narrow, how almost comically obtuse must appear the man who does so."

A7 (There's been such a clamour all about us, such an electric fear and anger that I could hardly hear him.) "Man's life, Mr. Ford, should be hung on the supple backbone of despair." (But that was a trumpet above the battle.)

"*Yet even the galley slave smiles at his conquest of the delirious sea; and the drowning suicide grips his straw in purple fingers. Over the recurring desolation of continents one man arises with the will to create an offspring superior to himself.*"

The father smiles at my eloquent and angry brother. "*This has happened, Dr. Ford, but has it happened for the best. Unconsidered hope has perpetuated a species which was condemned to eternal suffering by Michael's sword at the gates of Eden. God could be cheated of his revenge if the race would only will its own extinction.*"

"*It is neither to spite a dead god that man lives, nor to . . . nor to avoid trivial discomforts. 'Behold, I am that which must ever surmount itself.'*"

Tom is never in doubt, but sometimes his eloquence falters. Then he will always seal off the bleeding stump of a sentence with a quotation from his musty prophet of naughtiness.

"*But, Dr. Ford . . .*" We stare at Daisy in astonishment and I, at least, in admiration. Her bubble face is flushed with her own boldness, and her eyes are white and wide. "*Dr. Ford, it's through love that we surmount ourselves, God's blessed gift. It's wickedness to despise it. I love you, Dr. Ford.*"

I thought that I had known it before; yet it needs the spoken word to fix and certify the end, to chisel finality on the incredulous heart. That was my last frail quaver of youth, and now I'm as old as winter or this ancient priest. For years mean nothing after the death of the heart. And the father has bidden me despair, despair, despair. 'Spare!' Ah, could I, with that other priest say 'Spare!' in a golden echo, and know that my pearl is somewhere still untar-

nished. For I HAVE known my moments of entire conviction, **A7**
when the watched kettle boiled, when the ripening grape
fell at last. But I am the man who must for ever be beginning again, unravelling, demolishing, retracing. This is beautiful! Twice two is four. My name is Max! Repeat it and
repeat it.
"You neither amuse nor even shock me."
Lilly! No, no, Max, it's the voice of the grey moon lady
there, of the pious and virginal Miss Black. Yet it was HER
voice, too, yes, Lilly's; the voice of my dead demon wife.
Glorious unity in diversity, so strenuously sought, then
found in this, that Lilly and Miss Black are one! Immortal
savage virgin! Yes, and I can go much further in this transcendent vision, for here's Daisy so changed that she's Miss
Black in all but the accident of position, Lilly in all but the
accident of mortality. The girl's face is sunken, yellowing,
damp, and her eyes are thickening with mud, glinting with
green gold. Is it any wonder that she limps to the door and
leaves us?

A8　And she's fortunate in her escape, for indeed this subterranean room, airless, invulnerable to the sun, is no place for a sun-devouring rose. Poor maid, she had wilted almost to death before she left us, and the beaded sweat of the Underworld had sprung on her cheeks. Sweet Eurydice, it was my backward glance which lost you. Lost? Ah, but only to me; she dies only to me, for to herself the maiden's deathless. And this was my punishment because I would have fastened like a vampire on your body and sucked out all your young secretions to restore my youth. I'd have left you dry of everything but tears. For I'm an old rotten man, a salted fish, a dry faggot for the fire. Even in the vineyard time I was never that nut-brown young Dionysus, but a wan and angular Silenus smiling ineptly among his garlands.

"Mr. Ford, I'm terribly sorry I kicked you." (And yet the shame of your apology is worse.)

"That's all right."

"I'm not allowed to talk to strangers, but I suppose I can say I'm sorry to them. Besides, you're not really a stranger."

"Well, the kick certainly brought us together."

"Max Ford is pungently attracted by Mrs. Goodman, and Billy's got four cakes in his trouser pockets."

"Mr. Ford, sir, it was the dog! It was the dog who spoke!"

Good heavens, but it wᴀs the dog! And has it come at last, then, and have I crossed the frontier? Has madness come? "No, Billy, no, it was a trick of Mr. Parsley's. Don't worry, and don't let him see that he deceived you. But that little reassurance, as much for myself as for him, is all that I can give. Though he clamours now for so much more—even for a confirmation, as I guess, of his own dubious existence— yet childhood is my own disease and I must guard myself from any touch of it. May Max of the landing cupboard forgive me!

And now be calm. The silver kettle has thrown a sudden jet of boiling water on to my knee: but I make no cry or sign. I smile and mop my trousers with a snow-white handkerchief, while Tom's resourcefulness is proved again.

Well, it may be that this whole mad tea party has been an **A8**
object lesson (taught by some ignorant ass who thought I
had it still to learn). "We wish to show you how utterly you
lack your brother's presence of mind, his energy, his resolution." I can still smile brazenly within, and murmur the old
false consolation. 'We have our victories too.' Poor insubstantial little things, how readily they succumb to the oceans
of doubt, how timidly they rear their Ararat heads again!
I've sometimes dreamed of scales in which unlikes can be
weighed against each other. Two Victoria Crosses hold the
balance with one elucidation of a text. One thoughtful,
understanding word outweighs a hundred blind good deeds.
For without these scales all our timid values are derided.

And now we witness the exit of another performer. Leer-
ing, grunting—a little bit pathetic now—Charley shuffles to
the door, turns to shout a defiant "Boo!" from above it and
is gone.

Thus our unnatural circle is reduced. Where now are Daisy and her brother; whither this outrageous Charley? Certainly I share their impulse to be gone, to be away from here to no matter what uncertain destination, hell, purgatory or paradise, oblivion, or simply to the grizzled and inarticulate company of my club. Then can I say that what detains me now is only the web which she has spun around me like adhesive ropes? No, for there's something else, some expectation of an outcome to this party, of a climax, an epiphany, a revelation. . . . Shall I see it?

"*Pluck it out! Cut it off!*" My brother bursts with rage beside me, his lean, longing profile scarred with anger as he watches the old priest's convulsions. And indeed he's sick, my poor friend, bent double on his chair and snorting like an engine.

"Miss Black, is there nothing we can do for Father Morton?"

She turns to me with all the formidable deliberation she can summon.

"It's a sickness of the spirit, Mr. Ford. The Father lives in a waste of rotting souls, and his nostrils are full of their corruption. How should any man survive such a vision of decay and desolation!"

(Indeed that's quite as Lilly spoke, as she shrieked in the piazza!)

"Do you suffer from the same sickness, Miss Black? Do you find the path to salvation so unambiguous that you too can smell our doom in the air?"

"No, not as he does; not as a saint must. But in your case, Mr. Ford, I can read enough damnation in your face. I think I never saw such cowardice in any eyes before."

And Lilly said so too, and they are right. I've cried through forty years for that wise mother, the ultimate arbitress who'd say: "Now do this, Max! Here's the truth, and all the rest is false! Now come to hospital! Now swim! Now sleep for two hours on my lap!" The sick hope of a child.

This is beauty now, this ariel-melody, this shrill lamenta- **A9**
tion all about us in the foetid air. Is it from the great bronze
Laocoon, or Philomel from the dry vine-leaves in the corner?
It brings no freshness to the room, for it seems, indeed, as
foetid as the air it whines in. Why, Father Morton's whis-
tling! Yes, doubled on his chair across the table, his lips are
pursed, and from a foot above them comes this dangerous
warbling. I think we're all uneasy, but it's the poor ginger
imp who shows it most. How he bobs up and down beside
me, hands clapped to his ears and on his small face such a
ravished disgust and fear!

And oh, oh, what new unimaginable horror is this, barbed
and tangled in my hair, with a harpy's claws? Loose again,
I see a bat, wings rustling as it weaves about the ceiling.
Up, great Tom, the bat-catcher! Striking at the monster he—
doomed souls! has belted Miss Black with his cushion. But
now he floors it. Little flying mouse, soft, brittle, innocuous
creature in your broken convulsions on the carpet! As Tom
throws it through the window, Billy gropes like a bat to the
door and leaves us.

A10   So Miss Black remains, and Father Morton, Tom and Mrs.
Goodman. What a wilderness we are reduced to of the old
and ageing, for at forty Tom's now our youngest member.
Young Tom! For years he was that, the baby boy who bul-
lied me indulgently but feared the wild dignity of Francis.

Now had I been in the Hampstead room, I would have
said: "Francis, dear brother, you who were with me on the
shore at Margate . . ." But alone there it was his pride which
rode him, for our thanatic devils can take any disguise, pose
as any noble or generous quality. So then there was the bedroom and the whispering nurses, the knight's long corpse
with open eyes, and lip curled back on Dr. Wildauer's
golden tooth. And while I could only shudder on my knees
beside you, it was young Tom, the prefect, who loosened
the napkin from your fingers, and forced your grey arms
along your sides. It was he who lied at the inquest to win
a dubious verdict from the coroner, and he who had you
burned in the new chapel on the hill.

Now, Francis, I can tell you that nothing at all has happened in these twenty years. Truly life is finished at twenty-
three, for only achievement remains, a sad and brutalizing
compensation for our youth. Old Francis, I can tell you that
we died together from your bullet, and I wear these twenty
years as lightly as ghosts or paper hats.

Why, what long unhappy face is this, so bloated with
grief and knowledge? Francis in death's filthy inflation?
Max! Yes, it's my own face, stale and unsightly in the golden
mirror, telling me that it's long past time to leave. Up behind
me bobs the harrowed face of Lilly Black, thinner through
the looking-glass, poor Lady of Devotion. And we must
leave before the Christmas-tree is lit, before the fireworks.

"Don't go yet, Mr. Ford." He grips me with his wasted
hand as I move away. "My stick, d'you see, is cracked right
across at the ferrule. I wondered, could you mend it?"

"Dear Father, there was never such an unhandy man as I.
I push the two pieces together so, but—so—they fall apart

3:

again. My brother's the man for you. Goodbye to you, father.
Are you leaving too, Miss Black? Ah, not with me. Then
goodbye, Miss Black, and Tom, goodbye."
  No, my old spider, I know that I can't escape you through
this door. I'm your cocoon to feed on when you will. And
bending low and humble, dizzy with her scents and stinks,
I plant a hot kiss on her hot palm. She winks, and I wink
her rosy incest back at her. In some stale bedroom of a
station hotel, half-past three on a Sunday afternoon, the
things we'll do, Mrs. G.! "Goodbye, Mrs. Goodman, and
thank you a thousand times for your hospitality."
  Here I come, Daisy, Charley, little Billy! Francis, here I
come! This is the door I dreamed of at ten, at twenty-two, at
thirty; foresaw, foresaw and recognized at once. Now I shall
know.

B1 **Tom Ford** On scars of Cromarty where the sea clouds break and sheet all the heathered horizons—there I run with Chirry. We had our hardest winter in the huts on the shore, sailing north to Iceland at the turn of the year and west to the Hebrides at the first stir of the seed. Each year we've trekked further northward, acclimatizing our spare bodies to the conditions of a new meridian, our minds to the unnatural extension of the summer day, of the winter night; testing the behaviour of bacilli in every temperature and altitude. (At Cape Wrath I lay for three nights on the foreland.)

This decent lady in tweeds keeps highland heather in a corner of her room: paler and taller than any that grows south of Ness, I heard, as soon as I saw it, the thin roar of bees, the mewing of black-headed gulls, the stoney chatter of a corncrake. She is the mother in the valley whose third-born was stolen by the Picts and abandoned on the loch shore under Nevis. Returning after forty winters it is this youngest son who takes the long-untenanted chair, ruin of all earlier claimants. But hardly has he returned to make good his birthright when the Pole draws him northward again. She will stand, this Mrs. Goodman, waving from the garden of the white house among the pines, smaller with every step we take. And I shall turn with Chirry on the first horizon, to wave, to feel a single sharp kick of the heart, and then to hurry down into the next valley and away for ever.

Beside her now young Tillett sits, the dancer. He's as supple and taut as a wild cat, and young as a larch in April. Each small movement of his wrist, arm or neck, suggests another following movement, and another. So that each movement seems to be the beginning of a dance. Then why does this graceful boy evoke the sprawling body of Scott on the arete, the only worthless life I ever risked my own to save? (From Chirry's savage, salutory anger I learned that lesson well.)

Turning to the strong soft sun at the window I sneeze

with joy in its southern gold. In this warm room my northern strength is matchless and indefatigable. There, only Chirry is my master, galloping eighty miles in a night, splashing across the fords and up the sheer escarpments. For my own rivals in endurance, I have, not the boy dancer nor old fly-blown Max, but the gulls wheeling day-long over the cape, the arctic seals plunging in the estuary, the tireless cormorant and stag. So I yawn like a giant in this room; smile and stretch a giant's lazy arm to take the biscuit which Mrs. Goodman offers. A white bull on a field of coffee, an Ayrshire steer! Max takes the hare, the better to run from life and hide in the quaint form of his timid erudition. He was always the searcher of empty corners and treasureless caves, who missed the pearl oyster at his feet. Old Max of missed occasions and prodigious hopes.

Here comes my bonny bride, the sweet face in the lamplight, the sweet still figure to greet me on the highland platform. There's a clear blue eye which no cataract will ever film. There's a straight nose which will never swell and snuffle with a septic antrum. No girlish acne mars the round cheeks, and the round breasts are as firm as hard rubber. This is the spare rotundity I asked for, the light eye and the light step. I shall take Daisy Tillett, and she shall take me.

Now that his sister is beside him, Tillett seems even stranger. For if she is mine, and I know that she is mine,— then so must he be, and I must know it too. I never challenged a mystery more gladly, contrasted there to such a radiant simplicity. The lad shall be laid as plain before me as Daisy; as the daylight. And I shall know him.

No, no, Max; be dumb! I've known too well this poor old stutter for assurance, your tongue leaping and twisting to find a statement where there is none to be made. "Yes, yes, Max! I'm glad I came."

This Noel Tillett, then: this dancing boy with all his bloom and mystery: "Tillett, I feel sure I've seen you before."

"I've travelled much."

Yet his smile betrayed him, for then I saw the shepherd boy in Iceland, climbing the scar before me, turning with just that smile to call me up to the next ledge of the foggy mountain. And his quiet voice betrayed him, for then I heard the voice of McAndrew's son, as he stood smiling on the white concrete of his father's dam. And yet the eyes are always Scott's, whose screams among the falling rocks imperilled all my life and purpose. The proved inadequate, the pattern of all those damned dying who try to drag us with them. The shepherd and the engineer: the peril? In this young agile brother of my bride? Well, you may make any curious trinity you choose, but I shall box you back to unity. Oh, yes, I'll know you.

How would he be where the wind blows down from the

glaciers, and night falls from the mountains like an avalanche? How would he be where the tide comes in like wolves. I think he'd die in winter, with the summer migrants who delay too long.

And how will you be, fair girl of the south? I'll show you that the way of greatness is to find refuge in your worst peril, and I'll set you on Chirry's lustful back to ride the hills alone with him.

Now with a grave air she takes her biscuit; and soon she'll have need of all the gravity she knows. Her brother's face is sick and startled. His eyes gape wide at Mrs. Goodman. "Mrs. Goodman!" But my call alarms her and her hand has shaken. A teacup drops from her shaking hand, to break as softly as an egg on the thick carpet.

B3   Within my head the white house explodes in a fury of snow, as I turn to look back at it from the first horizon. And there before me in the pass stands the fanged wolf-woman of last year's dream, her talons raised, her grey lips still reeking from a feast of sons. She calls that I shan't leave her house, that I've returned to stay for ever, or she'll devour me here in the pass. War's declared, then, old fanged bristler of my dreams, old dragon at the treasure, old target for my levelled Mauser! Oh, but I know you. You were the monster at the spring. You were the ogress of the Yorkshire cliff. You were the Windmill Woman and Kurasha.

Yes, her yellow teeth are bared as she stoops to gather the broken teacup. Tillett has reeled to his feet beside her, green as a may tree, frail as winter bracken; now takes the pieces with a sobbing bow and trembles to the door. "Hi, Tillett, stop!" But my voice has been enchanted to a whisper.

All right, my shepherd boy, apprentice engineer! I'll stay in this windless room to raise a breeze for you,—to bring you back to us with a breeze from the south. Oh, you shall come back, my mystery, my dancer. Even now the air is stirring with snow and rotten leaves, tapping the heather against the wall, making Max shiver beside me. I sniff the winter for new enemies; and here they come!

Can you imagine that a mere change of background will be enough to disguise you! Old man of the Arlberg and the blizzard, who moaned ahead of us to the precipice edge. Old dying man in Ward 18, whose dying hand I nearly took.

And behind you comes your hired coot, your bald-headed clown, deriding you and paid to do it. What a vicious parody of a man this is, far nearer to a baboon or a chimpanzee! His whiskeyed breath engulfs me as he takes the chair beside me, and his mottled eyes roll around the table.

I've known you all for years: first knew you in the nursery by the river. So long ago the wolf was in the wood, and the ugly laughter crackled in the tree-tops. So long ago the old blind beggar screamed for pity at the gate of the public gardens, and crows were laughing in the sycamores. The dragon lay three times coiled about the fountain and the witch, Kurasha, flew above us in the windy sky. Can you think that I shall fear you now?

To you I gladly gave a certain little boy, young Tommy, with all his doubts and fears and impotent malignancy, with all his childish expectations. But as for me, have you forgotten that it was I who learned to know all your weapons and your plans, your wearisome manœuvre on the flank, the ignorant accuracy of your guns? She-wolf and old snow man, witch and clown and abandoned child! Spirits of the avalanche and flood, of the resourceful bacillus and of dry rot, mist and the midnight beetle!

B4   Poor recurrent victims of my rifle! Can you imagine that I shall be unwary in such a company; that I shan't watch every movement of your hands, every twitch of your faces; listen for every word or grunt or sniffle? Over this no-man's-land it's as still as the polar sky, and not a poppy bends or shivers. But I've known your silences and immobilities before:—the old priest in contemplation; Mrs. Goodman's teeth concealed by a sober lip; this Merry Andrew gorged and placid. Soon one Verey light will sing in the sky, and I shall hear the machine-guns rattle out their other-side-of-the-question, the cannon howl like an old dog for Pity, Pity, Pity. And the poison fog of "life's mystery" will roll along the floor and into every corner of the room.

"*Stir up the fire, Charley. My old bones!*"

(My old finger slips from trigger-guard to trigger.)

"*Old syphilitic bones!*"

Now to watch both from the corner of each eye, ready to fire from the hip, leap instantly round to fire again. There! A clatter behind me, and red embers are burning blue across the hearth. One instant only to—barge him away and —gather them, gather them—throw them back to the grate with fingers or shovel. Not even a scar on the rug.

And that's one attempt defeated, the first assault broken. But only one; only the first, so I must wait and watch as a runner crouched before a race. Watching, I find Daisy's shallow shining eyes. But I despise this sullying of action with a silly admiration, as if the action had been some schoolboy proof of manhood, a knight's idiot jousting at a tournament. No, no, my bride, it wasn't to win your love that I acted as I did, nor to exhibit my alertness, but to prevent a conflagration. And had McAndrew built his dam to win a woman or a bet, to drive away a complex or to prove himself, he'd have been no better than these midgets here. He builds because he wants a dam built.

Now Max is stirring in his chair beside me, burning once again with some new discovery of doubt, riding a night-

mare of temptation or perplexity. "Max, take her, take   **B4**
it, take whatever tempts you!" But he is buried too deep to
hear me, too deep in his turmoils of desire and fear.

No doubt he'll do it at last, so late that the desire will
have been long dead in him. And then what a wealth of
guilt, what a welter of self-examination! Poor Max! I remember the day when I found him sobbing in the landing
cupboard, and told him—it was the day of Francis's funeral
—that grief had been invented by a false god. He blubbered
there for two hours, shaking the stairs.

"Don't touch her, Charley!"

Unawares! Yes, they nearly caught me then. Now never
forget that recollection is a drug.

Touch who? What new attack have they prepared?

B5 It seems it was a private signal to summon reinforcements, for now a barbarous little head appears, squinting slyly round the door. Now Charley hoarsely confirms the order, and there we have it, the whole of it, the urchin in corduroy shorts, pasty with overfeeding. He advances sideways, with a dangerous diffidence, fingering his yo-yo. They often employ children as their agents, deftly turning the infant perversity to a more disciplined destruction, making their own assault behind the mask of childish innocence and weakness. This was the boy who looked down from the oak tree, his face filigreed by oak leaves, to misdirect me in my search for Chirry. There was the boy on the quicksands at Thurso, whom I DIDN'T rescue. I know them.

And therefore the instructed kick under the table was quite to be expected, and it's without surprise or anger that I rise to chastise him. There is a certain disgust in the feel of cold little ears under my palms, and in the toothy mouth opening to a scream of anger. Now Charley smiles and claps his fat hands. Mrs. Goodman bares her teeth again in a grin of blood, happy at violence inflicted anywhere. The priest looks thoughtful and approving. The boy himself has quickly dried his eyes, contained his sobs. He stares at me with a fag's eyes, adoring the athlete who has whipped him. So it seems that even my enemies are forced to recognize that I am the stronger and that Life must conquer. Already they contemplate surrender, and already. . . . Oho, my old fiends of the nursery and the snowstorm, was THAT your plan then? No, I'm not to be beguiled by your flattery, for you shall learn that I despise the trivial action no less than your false admiration of it.

I shall feel no warm touch of pride until the castle itself lies before me, across the wilderness of heather. I'll feel no pride until the old race is extinguished, and the moorland's converted to the garden of five rivers. There'll be no pride in me until disease is dead on our northern peninsula, and our dykes defy the sea. Those who praise us for our easy

triumphs are the worst enemies, however honourable they
may be, however beautiful. Now smiles are far more dangerous than anger.

This room is unbearably stuffy. Even the little boat in the aquarium by the window stands up as straight as a painted ship, no breath of a breeze in its sails. Call to the Greenland winds!

"*Repentance, what a blessed thing it is, Mr. Ford. All knowledge is in sin, and all virtue's in repentance.*" Parsley's harsh voice grates across the table, as he exhibits his power to do with Max exactly what he chooses. And where could he find an easier victim than my brother, one so confused and contradictory in his purposes? Only in this one clarity am I stronger, in the pin-point precision of my goal;—to push THERE, at that single premeditated point beyond the encircling frontier, forward from the railhead.

It's my brother's too heavy virtues which undo him, and not his unimportant vices. What is this "conscience", after all, but a great magnifying-glass held up to sin.

B6 And here comes old Conscience in person!

It's a woman, which is right; yellow and tubercular, which is right, for conscience is the consumption of the spirit, the jaundice of the mind. She walks with the firm carriage of disapproval, nods stiffly to her hostess-ally, sits down beside the child and instantly begins to whisper in his tingling ear. But the boy's swollen slavish eyes still dog me. Dog! An old slobbering retriever has followed the woman, flop, flop, flop with its feeble paws, and leaves a trail of filth behind it on the carpet. The beast should be destroyed. They know my rage for hygiene; know that I must turn my back on the turbulent table and leave them free to conspire there. Even as I bend my knee to scrape at the dungey detritae, I hear the serpent's coo behind me. *"I think I used to see you at St. Aloysius."* They attack me vicariously now, and at my weakest point. For should Daisy be destroyed, my labours would be all undone.

And it's clear that this was concerted between them, for now the old priest sidles into action, addressing me through poor belaboured brother Max.

"I've read your work with the greatest interest, Mr. Ford."

Now would it be wiser to listen and reply? Would it be better boldly to refute their poisonous talk, or boldly to shut my ears to it? Though God knows that boldness is no particular ambition of mine. I may need caution or even subterfuge;—indeed whichever quality gives the greatest promise of success. But I'll follow no quality, no, not the most heroic, for its own silly sake alone.

Now I hear old honey dripping from the poisoned comb, and I hear Max sucking at it like a child starved of calories. His eyes are greedy for the comfort of the false old man. Isn't he the very soul of wisdom, Max, and ah, what a courtesy and gentleness!

"The full man, the man of thought and feeling, cannot but be attentive to the many and beautiful distractions on his path. Straitness of purpose is not a virtue which I have ever

been able to esteem very highly." I'd say that in Max you preach to the converted, father, if I didn't know that in Max you preach at me. So old and sick a man (for now I see the tertiary symptoms blooming all over him) and yet so full of virulent energy! *"Giant Despair could have been turned into an ally, had he been treated with a proper respect."* And I know that one too, the daring paradox, the power of nonsense masquerading as a new revelation.

Now there's such a din between Parsley and some other disputant that even if I wished I could hardly hear the old man's purulent wisdom.

"It is possible, of course, to pursue some single ambition, and to neglect or deride everything which conflicts with it. But how pitiably narrow, how almost comically obtuse must appear the man who does so!"

Why you old fool, I'm not a child or a curio-hunter to be beguiled by that pleasant sunset on the left, the plum tree on the right.

"Man's life, Mr. Ford, should be hung on the supple backbone of despair." Oh, what a damned old man it is!

"Yet even the galley slave smiles at his conquest of the delirious sea . . ." (How fluently and easily it comes! But was it politic to speak at all?) ". . . One man arises with the will to create an offspring superior to himself."

Smile your sick soft smile at me, Father Morton! Weave me around with your melodious, despicable words! For they are mercifully predictable, my enemies, and nothing that they can do will ever surprise me; no sudden change of plan, no ambuscade or false surrender. *"If the race would only will its own extinction."* The syphilitic dotard!

Now the devil take this dumb stutter of anger! "Behold . . ." (old Zarathustra, old fighter, now spring like a prince to my rescue!) "Behold I am that which must ever surmount itself."

Oh, but it was folly to speak at all. They had prepared a trap of words, and I was caught in the horror of stumbling words. I'd be wiser to be as still and silent as a statue; and indeed I shall be.

"But Dr. Ford . . ." Yes, Miss Tillett! You too, Miss Daisy Tillett! Now I see that they nobbled you while my back was turned, and put that soft glow of treachery into your eyes. "I love you, Dr. Ford."

"The flushed irrepressible avowal!" (And can this be the voluble doctor who swore to speak no more!) "In a sense I am grateful to you, Miss Tillett, but I must warn you that you have become the instrument of certain seedy and murderous powers. Love is a reward at the end of the journey, but at any earlier point it's the offer of an enemy."

Pray, laugh yourself to death, Father Morton. God knows, you're near enough to it, and certainly your half-dead body offends me much more than anything that you can say. I'd diagnose that you're eaten to the edge of the grave by the microscopic furies, the spiral punishers. It needs only one smooth pressure on the needle to make you topple. I'd gladly be the agent of your cutting-off, most gladly rid the over-populated world of your plaguey body and more plaguey mind.

It may be that I've done the girl an injury, and that she was quite unconscious of the role they made her play. Yet guilty or innocent of purpose, it can make no difference to my action. All I know of her is that she tempts me to a fatal loss of powers; and therefore she's as much my enemy as any witch or clown.

Now she stands limp and defeated at the table, my scarred, unhappy bride. And as she walks, so she droops and withers like a frostbitten flower. "Daisy, stay!" But only a soundless whistle calls her back; and now she's gone.

B8 And have I failed then, in this departure of my bride? Or was it the necessary sacrifice;—Isaac burnt without reprieve to a greater God than love? No, it was a failure, for I should have kept her HERE subdued, awaiting the victory and its reward. Yet nothing, no, no, no, nothing is irrevocable until death; and failure is no worse than a delay, a pause, a hurdle to be jumped again. I shall win this Daisy back again, and win her to the bridal glow of her first arrival, to her uncorrupted innocence. I'll win back young Noel too, for mine must be the victory of youth.

When you killed Dickinson in the laboratory at Swindon, who recovered his notes and decyphered them through eighteen weary months? Who saved Harry Edwards, battling with frostbite in a snowbound hut? Who arrested the typhoid in Malton, after the floods, alone to take full responsibility for the untried serum? And this Doctor Ford, pruned of self-seeking, pruned of pity or conceit, was it to meet his Waterloo at tea-time that he worked and fought!

"Doctor Ford hasn't changed his underclothes since his last Himalayan expedition."

Even the dogs are given words to distract me, so magically savage and resourceful are my enemies. Get away, black dog's shape. What are my underclothes to you! It wasn't to be defeated by a dog's scurrillity that I came so far, by the false honied wisdom of a dying priest, by the threatening gestures of a cannibal hostess, by the spite of an adenoidal child, or the arson of a ham comedian. Ah, my poor Max, so it's you who must suffer now for this impotent rage against your brother. So! for the kettle which scalded your innocent knee.

"Oh, well done, sir! Well done, you practical fellow!"

You impudent bald buffoon! If once I had you on a glacier what I'd do. . . . Now restraint, doctor, for God's sake! Now be restrained, contemptuous and indifferent! I never come nearer to disaster than in these forgetful moments of anger. Heaven knows that ridicule is no new weapon, but I'll show

48

them that the last and loudest laugh is with the strongest **B8**
man. What a thunder of laughter that shall be, drumming
all the china in this room to pieces, rolling up the fiords like
a tidal wave!

"You've done more than your share of good deeds. I think
you're simply wonderful."

Good deeds, you whiskey-sodden ape! I, who left a nine-
year-old to scream on the quicksands, stood by to watch the
writhing body sucked away! I'll teach you how good my
deeds can be! I'll teach you on your buttocks and your
pate!

Now twice I've stood on the very razor edge between
survival and calamity; twice I've stumbled and swayed to
the left side in my nursery tantrums. But now I have
recovered; now I am vertical again and firmly planted. And
he knows it! And he writhes to the door like a fat snake
with a broken back.

B9   Surely this departure will mark the turn of the tide, high up, God knows, perilously high on the jetty wall. They drove out Noel and his beautiful, dubious sister; they toppled Max with the lazy flick of a straw; they've used fire, flattery and earth against me, dogs and clowns and scalding water, ridicule and gentle lies. And though one of them has turned his fat tail on the battlefield, many are still undefeated and maleficent.

The old priest still hurls his sickness at me like a glove, convulsed and belching on his chair. He flaunts this moribundity like a black banner of plague and reaction, as if to defy the whole sober faith of my medical training and experience. Only the needle remains. Oh, sterile purification of the needle! Grant that my chance may come to use it!

(In Granada once, in the bull-ring, among all the hard colours and under a hard white sky. . . . I never yet went further south. . . . The tiny hero poised his blade; thrust, and blood spurted from the matted, corrugated neck to drench his face and satin shoulders. Solitary initiate! The strength of God reborn in him. Yes!)

The pygmies say that we despise life, because we hate such travesties of life as this moving corpse here. They labour to preserve their rotted bodies to a racked end, yet they murder every giant who dares to surmount them. Oh, when shall we stand on the edge of the last desert, and stare like Cortez at the end of this pea-sized world!

"I do most strongly recommend these cakes to your attention, Dr. Ford."

Puffed with airy pastry, succulent with cream; pink, chocolate and almond paste; brown treacle, ginger, curranted and sugared, the whole plateful trembles in his hand. No, my syphilitic reverend, I'll take none from you!

"Then won't you try this Yorkshire spice-bread? You see how rich it is, quite wet with raisins and figs, dates and plums and farm butter."

"I've eaten enough, Father Morton."

Now what new disease is in the air, that Max should stare **B9** like a paralysed rabbit round the room, that Miss Black's gaunt head should thump on her chest, that the child should tremble and press his ears? This is the moment to watch every corner of the treacherous room; the door, the fire, the alcove there, the yellow ceiling. Watch the window! And a vampire swoops from the sky, claws at my brother's hair, tangled black in the grey hair, beating cold wings against his ears. Now it lurches free again, and flies blindly against the yellow ceiling. Strike, then . . . and miss (to shrill batlike howls of their laughter). Strike again . . . and, oh, forgive me, strike two birds with one cushion! Forgive me that it's I who laugh, Miss Black, discourteous avenger that I am. And goodbye, little savage, goodbye. Away you go together, boy and bat by door and window, blind little creatures of the night. And who shall mourn you?

B10

"Dr. Ford, you mustn't think that I resent your assault . . ." (All hackles up, Tom; fists, hackles and vizier up. Do I know this tone? I've known it in business men and cadging children, in grandmothers and dogs and students. Does it convince me of the lady's sincerity? It convinces me that her intentions are as evil as they are obvious.) ". . . I would like you to know that I do truly respect you as an adversary." (Ah, my witch!) "I think we both despise cowardice . . . . (You're wrong, for in an adversary I much prefer it. Who'd waste his time against courage if he could save it on a coward!) "Left to himself what does modern man ever do but burrow back into the slime he sprang from! We both know it, Dr. Ford."

"Whereas you would prefer him to kneel to a god of his own contemptible invention, a god who shares every one of his qualities, except, Miss Black, the saving one of existence. I have no respect either for you or for your faith, and I cannot conceive that further conversation would profit either of us."

Isn't that your cue, Miss Black, to cut and run. Then why delay, you old thwarted miserable thing?

Well, Francis, well! No, I've not forgotten. There lies your martial body on the bed, as I bend to take the napkin from your fingers. I took a torch from you when I bent there tearless, Max blubbering on your other side. And I've taken it further than ever you could have done, my old dead brother.

She rises at last, the conquered witch, with a loud clinking of rosaries and Peter's Pence, her crucifix swinging vertical and agitated on the blank black plain of her breast. Max stands before her, smoothing his bat-ruffled hairs at the mirror. And now he turns with his old stoop to smile at us. Ah, why should you accost him, for you must know that it's not his part to mend the stick, my old unhandy Max; my brother.

I'd wish him to stay. Yes, this brother has deserved some-

thing better than such an abject and ostentatious failure. At **B10**
times I've felt . . . It was this smile, I think, which recalls
certain rare smiles of the far past, when it seemed indeed
that TWO of us were needed. There was a keyhole where he
bent, talking of a passage filled with starlight and statues.
Such humbled dignity!

"No, Max. Don't say goodbye!"

And yet he makes his heedless circuit of the table, bowing courteously and taking leave. What if I should leave
beside him: yes, abandon everything and inexplicably
leave beside him. To CHOOSE to fail, at the very threshold of
my triumph!

Ah, no, Max, my last enemy. Go, with all your quaint,
stooping dignity, unwept. Kiss the moist maternal claw.
Now lift your professor's arms before you, and make your
suitable unmeaning exit. No more uneasy questions, never
answered. Confusion's all resolved in the night there, beyond the door.

B11 Now there's a sobbing behind these walls, the weeping murmur of women, somewhere muffled all around me. But not for Max. For whom?

Miss Black has kissed the Father's ring, and the ringed finger is leper-white. Behind his ear a suppuration bursts out, flows over the collar and across the black shoulder. The heavy nose subsides in ripe decay as I watch it.

"Father Morton, who was the young man called Tillett?" And the walls are suddenly singing.

"Bless you, bless you for your question, my dear boy. Young Tillett is my son of the flesh and the spirit, my Ariel son, my true and sole heir. It's for you that he'll come back."

"Father, let me take your stick. It only needed—that—to make it whole again."

"Allelujah! Allelujah!" sing the singing walls of women.

Now to hold tight my breath against the stench, thus to take him in my arms and very gently press the needle.

"He's dead! The father's dead! They've killed the father, killed the Church, killed truth, killed God!"

Oh, but you stayed too long, poor lady. Now she runs like a dervish about the room, stoops to bang her head against the wall, and to fall in a scream on her knees.

"He lives!"

My mother rises, and the witch crawls chattering away.

My mother rises, and a round red sun of the North has risen in the sky behind her head.

"Now go when you will, dear boy! Dear man!"

One green arm is held towards the open door, and far away in the house I hear the shouting of the exiled woman. ". . . killed truth, killed God!" But nearer and nearer come the quiet steps, the young steps, through passages and halls, upstairs and down them. Oh, come!

Now all the door's a green radiance about the standing body of Noel Tillett. A spoon stands in the tea-cup, and he holds this chalice like a star before him. His wide black eyes are caves behind the light, where all the glories of our future lie in state.

"Now, sir, I kneel to immortal man. I kneel to the end of night and winter, and to the pale sea of corn rising across our tundras. I kneel to the detonations of the thawing river, to the ice blocks flowing from the ice-bound harbour, to the spring catch of herring creaking the trawler's ribs. (For a breeze has filled those little sails.) Far up the scars, the snow is melting into torrents, and gorse bursts about us in a throng of gold. To-day the strangers will come to greet the season's change, young men sailing from the islands whose faces nobody knows. And I'm here, sir, still here, to show them how our little winter clinic has spread to a white spring city of the strong."

B12   He set down the graal before the mirror, and now he dances north and south, east and west about the room, scattering spring flowers around him as he dances. But I am kneeling, stilled and silenced by the glory. For this, my hands are scarred and scalded. For this, I conquered childhood and tamed the human mother, fought Pride and Pity. It was for this that I was harsh and graceless, hated by the gentle and deceitful, despised by the lovers of love and art. Now I may triumph over the blind dead. There were some who dreamed of a kingdom beyond the grave, where their shames and failures would be rewarded by indescribable bliss. Some boasted that posterity would never forget them. But their bodies lie rotted beyond resurrection, and their dead spirits are already forgotten.

I, and only I, can restore the dead to life. Here stands dead Tillett among the flowers, with his dead sister beside him. Her naked body shines in the starlight of the graal, and she smiles my victory and my reward. My mother has laid laurels on my head, and the women are singing the victory over Death.

Now the naked girl has knelt beside me, and Tillett lays a garland on her head. Her naked flesh smells sweetly of ripe apples, and her scent rises to me with odours of the spring. But soon she shall be kissed by heather and thistle, bathed in bog water and in the flooded burns, mother of the wind-tamers and the builders. Tillett has joined our hands among the flowers, and out in the garden the women are singing the birth of a city.

"Dear friends, by this act I make one flesh the Master of Life and the Maid in Bloom. By him her womb shall be rich with a furious progeny, eternal children of light . . ." Yes, to be the civic leaders of our city, taller to the northern sun than man has ever been before, furious for the blood and heart of their city. "You will be blest by happy laughter in the woods, and by children dancing on the shore. And one shall follow in his father's glorious footsteps . . ." Yes,   56 my third-born son shall set out with my blessing on his quest, shall take the perilous chair, extend our city northward to the sea, level the hills and irrigate the moorland. "He stands stiff and expectant in the shadows behind you, his face aglow with the anticipation of his glory." He shall be a swimmer and a biochemist, mayor of our city and chairman of the hospitals. He will banish cancer and tuberculosis from the city, found universities and schools, control the sunlight and the rain, devise a new code of civil law.

This shadow! Curious indeed that there should be a shadow cast by nothing, passing now across the very orb of his face. Or as if a violet stick or straw lay clipped to my pupil itself, diagonal across the iris. Blink it away!

If I had delayed the fraction of a second longer I make no doubt that the house would have been in flames. And then where would we be now! Where?

C2 ***Daisy Tillett*** Dear face, I knew you at the harvest, smiling among the grey beards of barley; and a sheaf of barley was gathered under each blue arm. Now bless me, lady of the cornfields and the orchards. All your summer room is ripe with the winnowed grain and with the gathered green of our south-eastern Eden, of the garden peninsula. From equinox to equinox I dream that the fruit and blossom hang together, plum under the dancing plum blossom, scarlet cherries fringed and winged with the pink of the tree. And all this is with us in the London room, as we watch the rosemary shiver in a breeze, and the sun fall deep into the peaches.

Dear Noel, too, who takes my hand below the table, as if he feared that I might be startled by such a company of strangers. "Don't fear for me, my dear. I've known this room since I was born, and our hostess even longer. There's nowhere in the world where I could feel so much at home." My gentle brother smiles and nods; then sighs. Why sighs? Oh, Noel, Noel, if we were alone, you know how soon I'd sing your sighs away. Always at a sigh I've known how to wake his dancing joy again, to sing his eyes into sunlight, to kiss his boy's cheeks to the scarlet of a god.

"*I've travelled much,*" he says, answering some harsh question from the man at the bottom of the table. How sweet and soft it is, my brother's voice, so warm with courtesy and yet so far away, as if from a hollow mountain or an old tomb. But tomb? How mad and foolish these quick thoughts can be, for what has my Noel to do, my fisher-boy, with age or burial? When I'm long dead and long forgotten he'll be no older.

Did I smile into your old grey eyes that you smile so strangely into mine? But now I know those eyes, thoughtful in the quiet room at Amberley as you spoke of man's lost and greatest quality of wisdom. And I, disagreeing, finding in love our greatest quality, yet could not contradict you as you wished. But here and now I'll say it, Noel and Mrs.   **58**

Goodman now beside me and here our palpable trinity of
love. And then you shall know it too: you shall be gathered
in our love, and find your lost wisdom in our eyes.

"Oh, thank you, Mrs. Goodman." A white bird flies across
my biscuit, such a bird as flew above the oak-trees when I
lay among the flowers of Enna. Thank you, Mrs. Goodman,
for the message of your biscuit, bird of love and freedom,
bird of the morning sky. Here are those woods again, and
river banks where the wet air is thick with thyme and cow-
slip. And over the hedge the tall ladies are playing croquet,
laughing, taking tea. And all the children are asleep at the
top of the house.

Then why do you look away, Mrs. Goodman? Why are
you afraid? Because a teacup fell and broke?

C3　Within my head a cry of lamentation, and all the bare woods echo the weeping and the crying. The shrouded woman walks in the dust, and tears fall on the dusty road. At a well she sits alone and stares into the blank shaft where nothing moves or shines. By the banks of the Nile she weeps, searching for the torn limbs of her Beloved; and on Golgotha she weeps beside the empty cross. Now her arms are raised to a terrible sky, and only the thunder answers. Ah, my mother! The wailing is for the forests, where the tamarisks grow not. My mother!

Yes, her cheeks are fallen and the white bone stretches the skin. Her hair is loose and rare about her shoulders. The fallen cheeks are still wet with tears, but the eyes are dull and dry, all tears wept away. Noel, my brother, my darling, why have you risen beside her chair, and why do you hang there like a dying flower? Why do you take the broken cup without a word, without a word to me, your sister. "Stay, Noel, stay, stay! Oh, Noel, stay!" He's gone and Daisy's lost. For the heart of our joy is taken, and we are left heartless.

A wind blows out of the tombs, a black wind smelling of earth and airless stone. It moves me, liquefies, and the terrible flow begins. Shame of my puberty, red river of blood and shame. And Max's gentle eyes have guessed it.

All the young flowers have withered in this room. The lillies creak and rustle in the wind, a fortnight dead, and the dead scentless rose petals are blown into the corners. Now here is the Witherer himself, old man of the winds and caves: bent and crabbed he comes to claim me. His bent head passes below the hanging gardens of withered flowers. Now, Max, fulfil the promise of your eyes, the promise you made me with your smile. Hedge me round with your wisdom; guard me from the old man and his mocking attendant, and you shall have my love.

The wind falls as they take their chairs, sitting (no, my Mother of Sorrows!) close to each side of me. It's death that sinks here in this calm, as a mist sinks from a wet windless sky. But this is Noel's chair, and nobody but he may sit here. "I'm sorry but you're sitting on my brother's chair." "Forgive an old man's infirmity, my dear. Should your brother return, it's impossible that I shall still be here." He speaks graciously, and there's a frail kindness in his smile. It may be that I've done him a foolish injustice. Yes, it may be. Then tell me, Max, with your unhappy eyes fixed far off on the books there, tell me what I am to think of the old sick priest, bowed and frayed beside me. But indeed who here, who now, who anywhere, can do as Noel does, can put his dear young arm along my shoulders, letting me smell the woodsmoke of his hair, the apple sweetness of his cheeks. No, nobody can do it—except one other. Yes, yes, there is one other. Jesus, Son of Man, how did I forget you in my need?

C4   Sweet Lord of the lake and sky, my boy, my master. Christ, my brother Christ, now come to my empty, breaking heart, my calling heart. Oh, come, as you would come among us in the catacombs, to dwell in our living sacrament and in the arched echo of our songs. How you shone like pearls in the eyes of our blessed deacon Gracchus, while the emperor's horsemen thundered above us in the sunlight! We gave many saints in that autumn of the edicts; but, dear Lord of Love, it was easier to endure the brazen armour, the brazen laughter, than to be so tempted to confusion in a strange room.

"*Stir up the fire, Charley. My old bones!*"

Poor good old man, how you quake beside me now! But what will he do, this muttering servant with the bloody eye, what will he do but mock you and betray you?

Flames of the sacrifice! Then must we burn here in the blue fire to witness to our love? But oh, not you, my darling and departed! No, no, not you, my living and immortal brother. Never die! See, see him now, my living brother come again like the Saviour to pluck us from the flames. Who doubts him now as he stoops to save us!

It's strange that I had thought so, that I had taken the silent doctor for my brother. But now I know this doctor for the destined Hero, some soldier saint, some George, or Martin with a Christian sword. In Noel's dear name he fights, after the vigil and the consecration, after the solemn vows to seek my brother and restore him. And now he'll guard me from the wicked confusion of this room, from the fire, from trolls, from the horns of the moon.

Then why should you look away from me with such a harsh impatience, as if to say that you had no time for gratitude, no time at all for love? What have I done to be so cruelly slighted? Is it the sick shame of my condition? Ah, why was I born to suffer this old reproach of the moon's touch, and become the tainted object of a saint's disgust? No, I won't be saved with his contempt on me. I'd rather die.   58

"I believe your breasts are nothing but two dear little   **C4**
snakes, curled up tight under your bust-bodice."

Stop him, Dr. Ford. Stop the dreadful muttering in my
ear. What have I done to be treated so!

"Your little nose was made to play an oboe. Lady, I'd
dance down the whole Morden-Edgware tunnel to your
oboe."

I shall remember the singing in the garden and the sleep-
ing children. I shall remember our singing martyrs, who
are now asleep. I shall remember sleep and song.

"I'd just adore to pick that musical little nose of yours.
May I? Oh, do say I may!"

"Don't touch her, Charley!"

I would indeed have died if he had touched me; and yet
my protector was away and silent. It was this good and sick
old man, an old priest of the Lord, who saved me.

Then were you sent to be my comfort, little boy, or that I should comfort you? "Now, don't be frightened, little boy. Come in!" But the fat, bad voice has barked above mine, and the child comes in for terror, not for love. For it's a room of terror now, and there's little love here.

Then what can I do to give the poor timid thing the little love there is,—my own at least? How he grabs at the cakes, poor hungry thing, and gobbles them!

No, you silly frightened child! Because the ogre shouted and all the room about him is full of fear, this fear has made him kick at Max and be grinning now at his baby victory. For how can he listen to love when fear compels him, when ignorant terrors fill his little heart. Now see him strut as Jack, and we are giants all about him. "I'm not afraid," says Fear, and makes him kick again to prove that it's a lie. But must *you* be cruel too? Oh, speak to him gently, and you could exorcise his little devil.

Poor boy! Poor punisher! Oh, yes, I know that the devil must sometimes be driven out with tears. And I know that it was for my sake that your cruel unwilling sword was out. But I remember a spring, far-off and half-forgotten now, when love had no need of swords, when there was nothing under the open sky to frighten us. Will you take me back there, to the lost spring when my mother was young with her sisters, over the garden wall?

But now his eyes are on the cross again, on the far hill where his Saviour hung, and these are the eyes of our deacon at the dark altar and of Noel in the forest. Shall I ever share that high vision of love, cross in the sky or the solitary shepherd dancing; heaven's golden stairs in the sky? I could share it if he would let me. I would share it if once he saw the love in my face, across the dark room, my face still golden in the vanished sun. Oh, see it! See my love here!

"The good doctor seems very far away from us just now."

"Yes, father, he's near to God."

"It may be so, my child, it may be so. Or it may be, that you're misinterpreting the glow in our hero's eye."

"No, father, no. He sees love in the sky."

"True love, my child, is love of God and of God's holy order. But we cannot attain to that without knowing first the power of merely human love. Heavenly love is a transcendence of human love, and how can man transcend what he has never known? Now Dr. Ford—you need only look at his face to be assured of it—has never loved man, woman or child."

"I was vain and silly enough to hope that he would love me. But oh, I know now that it was vanity and folly."

"No, child. It would be a great sin in you if you were to lose that hope, for your love will give him something far more precious than the strength he worships now.

And without it he can never see the vision which you imagined in those unvisionary eyes."

"Then, father . . . ?"

"Then, my daughter, it shall be both your duty and your joy to win Dr. Ford's love. It's no time for modesty, child."

And in his old voice, though it quavers, though it sometimes trills like a blackbird's, there's an authority which makes me think it possible. Yes, he SHALL love me.

Is it that wasted face again? But when did she come? And why did she come, if not to torment me as she has always done before? Poor forsaken woman of the wilderness, who cried for Noel's death in the name of Christ, and would have killed them both. Now it's on Billy that she fastens her sad talons, and on her own thin heart as well. For both must die in the poisoned love of that embrace.

"I think I USED to see you at St. Aloysius."

So it begins again, the old tired quarrel of broken words and hearts, and of broken bodies. So, to keep her dark loveless faith about her, she lies and smiles, and smiles and longs to kill. So she threatens me with the blue talons which have scarred the cheeks of lovers since first the mitre rose among us like a sword. Oh, the old evil words! Can you believe them as you say them? ". . . you trusted your own unlimited wisdom for the proper employment of your love!" I trust the open heart, and nothing else. See, poor tormented woman, what you have done with my brother Jesus! The wicked folly of your worship; to drain His blood away and set Him on a golden throne, a mummy prince ruling stern palaces with the whips of dogma. But did you think that you could drown the sun, bring down the dancer, turn back the leaf into the wood?

"I know, Miss Black, that the devil speaks as you do now."

And I know that when his name is spoken aloud, he can't afflict us any more.

"*Straitness of purpose, Mr. Ford, is not a virtue which I greatly esteem. It has no use, you see, for the harrowing joys of human love. It allows no time for the contemplation of religious truth."* It's to me that he's speaking, bidding me remember that this saint indeed shall love me, love me, love me, a whole night, a whole life, with soul, heart and body. And together in the morning we shall serve Him at the quiet altar, blessed in our love of the Lord and of each other.

Now the troll is barking in the wood again, and I must leave the green moss where I lay with my love. *"Ladies— Miss Black, Mrs. Goodman."* His red troll's eyes are like a wolf's in the forest. *". . . this ungrateful little monster here dislikes you both with all his horrid little heart."* Now all the red spirits are loose in the woods again, burning and shouting and dropping hatred into empty hearts. There fear stiffened into hatred. Here hatred curdled from despair. And now the sounds of hatred are as loud as a battle in the sunless room.

C7 "What is it, Billy? What's the matter, dear?"

But no: Fear never listened to Love. He turns away his trembling head, turns back to the loveless woman. And he's hers for ever. For what have I done with my love but dream of it, and waste it, dreaming away from the difficult action of love? Dear Noel, I'm but the ghost of a girl without you. "*. . . one man arises with the will to create an offspring superior to himself.*" The face of my love is all crags and valleys, lifted like a wild landscape to the sun. And this is no ghost heart beating in me here, rising to such a height that I can hardly breathe, filling my breast and womb. Oh, my love and my stranger! Call me once from the hills, and I'll dance to you. Love me all a night with your body and heart. "*Behold I am that which must ever surmount itself.*" And rise to what? To what wild hilltop? To what new race of giants? Oh, to love, my Tom, for who can rise higher? Nobody says it, for nobody dares to answer the sun of his eye, the sharp defiance of his voice. But I shall answer, for love was never afraid.

"But Dr. Ford . . . ?" (No, love is never afraid, though the heat of his eye is burning my face. Dear Noel, NOW!) "Dr. Ford, it's through love that we surmount ourselves, God's blessed gift. It's wickedness to despise it. I love you, Dr. Ford."

No, I won't hide. It's no use to burn me with your eyes, for I shall never hide from you.

"The flushed irrepressible avowal! In a sense I'm grateful to you, Miss Tillett, but I must warn you that you have become the instrument of certain seedy and murderous powers. . . ."

It's enough. That's enough. How curious that I should have. . . . For this wasn't fire but ice, and now, alas, all my poor body's fixed in it. Can I move? Yes, very slowly—so!—raising my right hand to my hair; rising; pressing the left hand on the table. But what snow-girl's face is this, of yellow backyard snow, now melting at the eyes and neck? Poor   68 dear! The children must have pelted her with snowballs. No, it's not Daisy, not Daisy Tillett! It's not the girl who looked so pretty in the spring, by the river of Enna, under the trees. Oh, yes, it's Daisy's face.

How innocent and busy they seem from up above them! I never thought that I should be the first to go, but here's moonlight on the ceiling, and I was to leave at the first moonlight. Hark, that's the troll again, barking far away on the hillside, under the pines. But I'm not afraid of trolls or moonlight. Here's my home, under the moon, in the dark of the forest where the old witch is praying for the troll.

Round the next corner of the ride I'll find him, dancing, Dr. Noel, dear brother with the crags and valleys on your face. Sweet Tom Tillett, here comes the Bride of Christ. Be ready to receive her kindly.

D3 Charley Parsley She's nothing but a womb, to be blown up like a jester's balloon and banged about at the end of a stick. Crump! Jocasta! Crump, Mary Mother of God! Crump, Ishtar and Cybele and the West Stafford Maternity Home!

Here we come, then, Nuncle and his Fool! Here I stoop and groan and belch, like my old syphilitic governor. "How low!" says that face. "Gives me the creeps!" says this one. This one's Ruth among the alien sugar-beet, soaked and coated with the juice of the root. She's the Spirit of Diabetes, killing with her superabundance of saccharine. She's a sweet girl, Miss Muffit, but there's a spider on his way, if she knew it.

Fee, Fi, Fo, Fum! I smell leather underclothes and a sou'wester, an airedale and a rump steak and a gale-proof pipe. I smell lysol and scurf and clean living. The Truly Strong Man: a fœtus smoking fisherman's plug; a baby gamekeeper who shoots on sight; unicellular, however you care to put it. An airgun! Yes, a great big airgun for your first term at the big school. The Truly Strong Man: after twenty years of preparation, he threw a gorilla over St. Paul's cathedral, smiled, brushed his hams and died in the gutter. He was the first to swim the North Atlantic smelling of coal tar and pipe tobacco: tested on landing, the aroma was found to be as strong as when he dived from New York harbour. They dissected his stomach, and found it stuffed with raw seaweed and seal's flappers.

D4   Long-face smells like the best of this bloody bunch, though every inch a boo-hoo and a breast-beater. He's a morsel of something rare and tasty, quail or sturgeon, but a bit tainted, a little bit "off." My, but he's sensitive! My, but he has high ideals, but my, how he fails to live up to them! And then, oh, my, my, my, how ashamed he is! The Sincerely Weak Man:—he was sick for shame all over the tart he'd paid two guineas for, and long before he'd had his money's worth. He was as pleased as punch when they told him he'd got the death-wish, but he never dared to wish hard enough. He caught a pussy-cat, pulled its tail, kissed its poor tail better.

"Stir up the fire, Charley. My old bones!" Old syphilitic bones! You gaga old primer of elegant wisdom, why does your little Charley love you so! Now you REALLY stink, you old corruption, you sweetheart! Scatter the embers ("Bugger!") and . . . watch intrepid Airgun rush into the breach. That's my level-headed constable! That's my prompt surgeon! Upsa-daisy, and back into the grate fly all my bad intentions. A wash-out! Why didn't I fling a live coal into each corner of this poxy room, into each poxy eyeball.

Let's imagine there's a toad under every chair, breathing like a grampus, just waiting for the word from me. Then come on, toads, put on incorruptibility, all forward together against the ramparts of the human condition!

I can smell out love here; or isn't it the racier stench of sexual rivalry? Got it! Airgun and Weeper are both after this drooping sweet, dewey sweet, honey sweet, sweet, sweet little Muffit. Weeper wants her lactic bubs to weep on: Airgun wants his brow stroked after a dirty day in the lab: girly wants Airgun 'cos he's REAL, but she'd like a reading-list from Weeper. So Airgun gets her, and won't she be in heaven, whipped round the North Pole, yelping with love as she skips! Now for a snarl!

"I believe that your breasts are nothing but two dear little snakes, curled up under your bust-bodice."

She jumps like a peppered beater. Now, this is good. I've   7:

got my Sugar on the run, and it's quite in vain that she **D4**
moons her mooey pools around the table. Airgun's planning
a stratospheric ascent in search of microbes. No time for
Sugar, so—have at her again! But this is very good. She's
showing quite an honest fear. Knock all the icing off a girl
and there's always a dear soft little kernel of terror, nestling
at the heart, as pink and succulent as a newborn squirrel.
Why, it would give me real pleasure now to pick a little
black moany out of that pretty nose. "May I? Oh, do say
I may!"

"Don't touch her, Charley."

O.K., Governor, O.K. Your heaviest whim is my command.
And, of course, you're quite right, Governor. The girl's a
blood-bath.

D5   Oh! Boy, a boy! That's my bishop for the Feast of Fools. That's my savage. "Come along in, Billy!" Come in, you snotty little swine, rancid with the polymorphous perverse, stiff with original sin. I love a proper little boy, gluing up the lavatory seat, putting flypaper in the invalid port, spying on Nanny's misbehaviour in the bracken. Suffer little children to come unto me, and, by hormones, I'll lead them against the shameful citadels of puberty! Ah yes, it's a natural child. I can read it in his honest vicious eyes: it's a jungle child reared on the milk of baboons, a masturbatory little man.

Bully, but that's my boy! He's lashed out under the table like a dromedary and caught the Weeper a whopper. Goody! he lashes again and all the lost horizons are wiped off Airgun's face. By God, there's no holding him! What a grin! What a scowl! What a squint of the devil!

And that's a good disciplinary doctor! Box his little ears, doc! and howl, Billy, like an angry porcupine! Fur and quills are flying, and all the little red demons are dancing on the table. But oh, no Billy, no Billy, no! You shouldn't slaver at your chastiser like a whipped puppy, or like this goggling Muffit here.

"Now kick the nice young lady, Billy."

Och, what's the use! Nothing could stir them up here but a tornado, and even that would be Airgun's opportunity. Fed up to the teeth and ready to vomit, that's Charley.

Now there's a polite and friendly Weeper!

"Charley Parsley is my stage name, but in private, Charley Morton. Your poodle, Mr. Ford."

He misses that, the literary old dear, so startled that a father should be a real daddy too. Now I confess that I haven't much heart to ruffle him. The poor Weeper's done for, and I guess he knows it. I'll prod him a little: then leave him for the Governor. ". . . he's a great man, Mr. Ford, though I say it."

"Well, yes, I can believe it."

"And can you believe something else, Mr. Ford. Mrs. Goodman—come a little closer—used to be a prostitute in Colwyn Bay. Twenty years from the squire to the pox."

"That can't interest me, Mr. Parsley."

"Ah, but she's repented after her fashion. Repentance, what a blessed thing it is, Mr. Ford. All knowledge is in sin, and all virtue's in repentance. I may say that the Governor is absolutely at one with me on this. 'Without sin,' he says, 'the world would signify nothing.' Oh, you'll appreciate the Governor. When he's free I'll have you meet him."

The good old Governor's got off with Sugar now. He keeps a sweet tooth, the old billy goat, for all that he's falling to pieces. I'd give my balls for him to win her, dose her, teach her the pleasures of love.

And here's another one; a tallow candle, a woollen stocking, change of life and a rosary. Or, sniff! sniff! yes, the hare and the broomstick, vervain and a rotten moon. It's Aradia her old self, disguised as a papist parishioner. Wicked harridan, and just the girl for Charley! He's my type, too, the old slobberer, dragging his fat paws across the carpet. "Here, sir! Come here, boy!" It's the very spirit of idleness and gluttony, bought to compensate the harsher vices of his mistress.

A good entry this, a fine performance. Her trunk waved in the air to trumpet her sanctity and our stink. What a black-hearted marvellous bitch!

Now our Hercules-Airgun is bent on one knee, like a dubbed knight, scooping up the tarry dung which doggy left behind him on the carpet. His face is like the backside of a mandrill, purple and crimson with the shame of it. I'd make all his tasks as shameful, oblige him to cock his leg against each of the royal palaces in turn, from Buckingham to Balmoral.

And now that Aradia's settled in her chair she bares her teeth at Sugar. More fur to fly, bless them, dear youth against dear middle-ages, dear sweet against dear sour.

"Mr. Parsley, will you make a bow and arrow for me?"

"To shoot what, dear child? What to kill?"

"Oh, anything. Cats, probably."

"Why not shoot Mrs. Goodman, little Billy. I believe she'd go pop like a balloon, with an awful stink."

"All I want, really, is for you to be nice to me. I'm so frightened. I don't like Miss Black, and I hate Mrs. Goodman."

"You trust me, little Billy, and I'll be nice to you" (after my fashion).

"*I know, Miss Black, that the devil speaks as you do now.*"

Oh, Sugar! Oh, golden hypocrisy of youth, I suck you like an acid drop. Such tart salivation it is, to taste the blue-eyed murderers, the gallant little honies, the bullying Davids and Temeraires.

The Governor's working on the Weeper now, and as **D6**
happy as a king. Weeper's, oh, so touched and impressed by
the sad wisdom of the venerable priesty. I suppose you know
best, guv, but if I were you I'd sting Weeper into a frenzy
of lust and make him commit an outrage on Womb.

Now for little Billy's hash!

"Ladies, Miss Black, Mrs. Goodman! Now that you're
both unoccupied, your undivided and indignant attention,
please. It's my duty to tell you that this ungrateful little
monster here dislikes you both with all his horrid little heart.
Ladies, I leave the punishment to you." (Aradia seethes like
one of her cauldrons.) And with this goes such a vile gri-
mace for Billy that he nearly tumbles backwards off his
chair. That'll teach him to trust a grown-up human! Yes, it
was a sweet job, a sweet job. Give Charley a hand, boys!

"*Man's life, Mr. Ford, should be hung on the supple back-bone of despair.*" Oh, you old rascal, you wicked old beauty, you; what the devil are you up to now? Oho, it was THAT; it was Airgun you were after. Hear him going off now like a sub-machinegun—pop, pop, pop, pop, pop! And what high-fallutin' cock it is, what balls-aching crap! "*. . . the will to create an offspring superior to himself.*"

Now that would be close to my heart if he meant what I mean. I've always fancied myself as a breeder of new hybrids, and my imaginary intimates are the Porcupard, the Serpephant, the Liomel. I've even coupled with a sow and been so optimistic as to engage a midwife for the far-rowing. What a lovely mongrel I'd arrive at—something with the courage of a rabbit, the speed of a tortoise, the amia-bility of 'a shark, the wisdom of a canary, the beauty of a warthog and the honour of a man. For though we're all vile species, each has ONE quality which pleads for it and pre-serves it. Humans are brainy—so much for them—and it keeps them going, damn it!

It's high time for another crack of the whip. A flea's circus, that's what this tea party is, and I'm the ringmaster. Crack! and Weeper pounces on Womb. Crack! and Airgun kills a dragon. Crack! and Billy sticks a pin into Airgun. Crack! and . . . "*I love you, Dr. Ford.*" Just so! Sugar's cue! I love you, too, Dr. Ford, I'd tear off your tits like scabs and plant embryonic rats' tails in the wounds. In fact I'd plant tails all over you; rats' tails to tassel your breast; two tigers' tails where tails should be; squirrels' tails for hair and lizards' tails on the backs of your surgical hands. Cocks' tails would make a luminous cache-sex. Dr. Ford, I'd love you even more, betailed like that.

And now for Aradia, heigh-ho. "I most sincerely regret Miss Black, that my intervention in regard to Billy was so unwelcome to you. The more so, since I am assured that we are at one in faith."

"That strikes me as improbable."

"You have known suffering, Miss Black, and known its value. Let me describe to you my sensations at the time of my anal abscess; what I sometimes call, in the fullest humility, my crucifixion. (A poor thing, Miss Black, but mine own.) A pain in the arse gives the added ecstasy or acute humiliation. I . . ."

"You neither amuse, nor even shock me."

"But you quite mistake my intentions. We are agreed, I take it, that God is a tiger. What more natural than that He should wish us all to suffer, or more honourable in us than to accept his pleasure with a ferocity equal to his own. Let's go thumb-screw each other, Baby!"

"I shall pray for you, poor creature."

You will, dearie! You'll pray for the addled soul of poor Parsley. Well, if prayers could kill, I'd be garrotted in my sleep to-night. (Bully, there goes Sugar!)

"Here, sir! Come here!" It's only your arrested stage of evolution, Rover, which makes you more tolerable than the humans. Sprout a soul and you'd be just as vile as they are. It's a nobly stupid cranium, isn't it, boy? I press the little islands of soft fur at his eyebrows: I pull down the kipper-coloured jowl, where his fangs still flash as white as a wolf-cub's. What a furrow bisects his scalp! How loose and nerveless the flesh hangs at his neck! Here's a cake, boy: and another! Here's a dainty slice of bread and butter, and here are lumps of sugar—six, seven, eight! Now let me hear you talk, sweety.

"Well, Rover, what do you think of the company?"

"My mistress, though it's the last thing you'd expect at her age, wets her mattress nightly."

"Come, come, Rover! You exaggerate."

"It's God's truth, Charley. And Dr. Ford hasn't changed his underclothes since his last Himalayan expedition."

"What a dog! What a dog!"

"Max Ford is pungently attracted by Mrs. Goodman, and Billy's got four cakes in his trouser pockets."

"Now, not another word, old boy!"

Did we shake them? No, they're past shaking. Oh, but I should have been the Atlantic ocean, to crumble the Empire State Building on to the heads of the Yankees, and Cardiff Town Hall on the fat behinds of the Welsh. Mighty ambitions and fat incapacity will end me in the loony bin. All I ask is uranium and the secret of its use. The things I'd do!

Now watch him! He's on the scalding kettle like a panther on his prey. "Oh, well done, sir! Well done, you practical fellow!" By God, I've truly stung him; yes, I have! His nostrils swell, and a streak of mandrill suffuses his cheek. Follow it up; follow, follow, follow! Just watch our Airgun hop! Watch our Jason struggling with his impulse to bash in yours truly's skull like an egg shell! "You've done more than your share of good deeds. Yes, I think you're simply wonderful." Oooo! Sir Lancelot, you frighten me, you really

do! Here I come! There's my bald skull for you! Crack it
open, doc; now do!

By Jesus O'Christ, Charley, but what great purple baby's
face is that? What hooded eyes? What a squatting toad for
a nose? That's Charley Parsley in the flesh, and badly in
need of a scotch, or, say, eight. Now, I had no idea it was
so bloody late, or I'd have . . . God knows, I've had my
fill of it.

Well, I did my best. I sent Sugar packing, and I gave little
Billy a crack between the eyes. And I'm to be prayed for—
Brrr!—by Aradia dear. Dogs and bitches! Dogs and bitches!
Leave 'em, Charley. Shoo! Off with you! You don't BELONG,
old boy. So off I march to the door with a cocky waggle of
the buttocks. "Boo!" to the filth of you.

E5 **Billy** I know that face. But no, I don't; I don't; I won't and I won't look back again to see. "Come along in, Billy." But why SHOULD I·come in! Oh, why SHOULD I!

Indeed, it IS Mamma's face. Oh, no, but it can't be: I know much better than to think so. "Your mother has gone away for a long time," said Mr. Wilkinson in the drawing-room. "She may never come back," said Aunt Ella in the garden. "Your mother's dead," said Harold on the beach. So I know all about it and you can't deceive me. She's deep underground with a stone above her and a glass dome of flowers. How I hate them!

But I don't care. Why should I care? There are plenty of cakes, and nobody to say a thing. I don't care, and I'll hoof them to show it. Hurrah, for he howled like a puppy. And that's for you too, you silly old man. How I hate them!

No! No! No! No! No! "If you dare to touch me my mother will. . . ." Oh, but they're broken, my poor little ears. Then I'll kill him. Yes, biding my time I'll have a terrible revenge on him, cut him to pieces, pull out his tongue and his teeth; I'll: . . . And everybody smiles, for they're glad of my pain. You too, you with the face of my mother, smiling all your big teeth at me.

He must be a boxer to be able to hit me so hard. He looks like a tiger-shooter and a channel swimmer. Does he mean to climb Everest one of these days? I'll go too. Yes, I'll follow him through the blizzard and the avalanche, over the crevasses and up the windy chimneys. "Sir, will you take me?" But oh dear no; he won't listen to Billy.

I'll take the chocolate éclair now (that's my fourth!). And still there's nobody to say "No more"; nobody to say "Where are your manners?" nobody to say "You're a very greedy little boy!" No, nobody cares what I do. So I hate them.

In the glass tank a little sailing-ship's becalmed: it's as still as a ship in a picture. "I say, you know, she won't sail without a breeze." Don't think that your silence makes me unhappy! I remember the storm, and spray on the drawing-room window. Who's afraid! And I know all about Mother Sharpey who locks little boys in her windmill on the hill. Who's afraid of old Mother Sharpey? And I know about the Black Knight who slays on the starless mountain. Who's afraid! *"Twenty years from the squire to the pox."* And oh yes, I know all about that Terrible Joker who shakes the hills with his wicked laughter, and makes the houses fall. But I'm not afraid of a Joker. I know about the Weeper too, and how he floods the valleys with his tears, drowning ten thousand. I'm not afraid of a weeper; no not I.

And I know about the stinking old Ogre of Sunderland who throws the pilgrims over the cliff, and then flies down to eat their bodies off the sea. You can't frighten me, you old ogre. In fact there's nothing here to be afraid of, and all of you must know that none of you can frighten me at all.

Yes, yes, yes, and I know Kurasha on her broomstick, with snakes out behind her in the wind instead of hair. Oh, where can I run to? Where, where? Or she'll hang me dead from the oak-tree, and I shall be food for her cats.

"What's your name, little boy?"

Never tell, never tell; you must never, never tell your name! "Goodness, child, don't be shy. I'm not going to eat you." Yes, she'll kill you and cook you and eat you and give what's left to her cats. Will nobody help me? Won't anybody save a little boy! Take the cake she offers, but look away and never tell, never tell! "Now speak up, child, please!"

"My name's William."

Who told? William told. Then, William, you're Kurasha's now, Kurasha's little boy to do with as she pleases. Now you can't move because of the spell she's cast on your secret name. You see! You can't move.

But there must be somebody in this room to save me. There must be somebody who knows a charm against Kurasha. Whose white magic will free me? Whose?

Yours, with your smile for a charm?

"Mr. Parsley, will you make a bow and arrow for me?" He winks when he talks, meaning "Just you wait," meaning "Don't be afraid," and "I'll save you, Billy!" How blue his big eyelid is when he winks! "Why not shoot Mrs. Goodman, little Billy. I believe she'd go pop, like a balloon, with an awful stink." I was right you see. He hates that lady too, and he'll hate her much more when I tell him how cruel she's been, pretending to be my mother. This is my friend and he'll take me away.

Yes, he'll take me away to his house by the sea, under the trees on the cliff. He collects shells, as I do, and has much better ones than mine, green and ruby and deep-sea shells. There's a gun for him and a gun for me, and seals are what we'll shoot, and strangers. In his yacht we'll go out fishing, to catch cod and conger, whiting, plaice and dogfish. He'll teach me to swim. He'll teach me to box and to fence.

Peaches grow in the garden, and figs, and I'll make a house in a tree. We'll eat crumpets and shortbread and ices and shrimps; scrambled eggs and chicken, trifle and jelly and pies. We'll stay up till midnight. We won't say our prayers. We'll sing as loud as we choose. *"Ladies, Miss Black, Mrs. Goodman. . . ."* Now he's going to tell them, and ha, ha! what a shock it'll be to them. Just listen now, listen! *". . . this ungrateful little monster here dislikes you with all his horrid little heart. Ladies, I leave the punishment to you."*

"Oh, what a joke, Mr. Parsley. What a good joke!" He likes to make fun of them, to make silly fools of them.

But the black, broken teeth are gnashing now, and his breath is stinking flame. "Save me, save me from the purple ogre! Oh, somebody save me!"

"What is it, Billy? What's the matter, dear?"

But silly girls are never any good.

"I'll tell you why you don't like me, William. It's because I'm the only person here who cares what happens to you . . ." Because you want to take me away to your house in the wood. Because your eyes are yellow. Because your grey cats are as large and hungry as wolves. "Won't you come and see me sometimes, and I'll tell you what God wants you to do? You'll come, won't you, William?"

"I was going to live with him, with Mr. Parsley. He told me about his house by the sea where nobody could hurt me and where he'd teach me to swim and where we'd eat. . . .

"Oh, William, child. Can you believe it?"

No, and not you either. No, nor anyone at all. All I believe is that everyone hates me; so I hate them back. But oh, if Mamma were here she'd chase you away in a trice, shoo you away with her great green umbrella. There's not one of you here who could ever frighten my mother. She laughed at Kurasha and the ogres, at the Black Knight and the Weepers and the Jokers. Who ever saw Mamma afraid of anyone.

(Pocket the cakes now! Pocket them quickly!)

He smiled and said I was to trust him. But then there was an ogre behind his smile. She tells me that she cares for me, but it's only to make me come away with her, only to make me belong to her. His house is a black house on a big black rock beside a black sea, and nobody, no knight, no airman, ever comes there. Her house is a green house in the beards of the forest. And I'll not go to either of them, no, not I.

Take your horrid smile away! I know you hate me. Don't dare to smile like that at me, for I know my mother's dead. Yes, I know more than you, or any of them, think. Listen: "It was in winter that she died, and snow covered the garden. The doctor blew on his hands as he walked across the snowy garden from his car." (I whisper because nobody answers when I talk aloud.) "And then I was sent away while they held her funeral. She was buried under a stone, and I shall never, no, not if I live to five hundred, never see my mother again." You see that I'm not the silly little boy you thought me.

Now the old one bends towards me, and pfuff! what a smell he makes of wet earth and dog's mess. Oh, Mamma, my only dear one, what can I do now to be safe, for it was only on your lap that I was safe?

"She's your mother, my boy."

"She's not!" No, you smelly old clergyman, she's not my mother. I see Mamma's grey earrings and her muslin collar; I see the black bun behind her head. But that's to make me believe it—as if anything could make me believe it, you silly fools! She does it to frighten me, that's all.

As a matter of fact my mother loved me more than any boy has ever been loved by his mother before. She often said so. If I was out of her sight for a minute, she was anxious. We walked hand in hand through the tall bracken on Ray's Moor, and sometimes she bent down to kiss my head. Once we took the cliff train to Dover and walked through a storm to the castle. She sat on my bed, singing "A Birdie with a Yellow Bill," and the big blue beads of her necklace hung down to stroke my chin. She never left me alone in the house, never once. From Old Mother Sharpey she held me tight in her arms. From the Black Knight she kissed my head. From the Ogre of Sunderland she tucked me up at night. From the Terrible Joker she gave me eucalyptus and a hot-water bottle. From the Weeper she left a nightlight burning by my bed.

But YOU'RE not the Weeper, sir. Oh, no! Now I know what it is. You're sad because you're lonely, having no son to comfort you, no little boy to live with you. "And anyway, you're not really a stranger."

"Well, the kick certainly brought us together."

"Max Ford is pungently attracted by Mrs. Goodman, and Billy's got four cakes in his trouser pockets."

And it's true. But how did he know? Oh, how did he speak?

"No, Billy, no. It was a trick of Mr. Parsley's. Don't you worry; and don't let him see that he deceived you."

"Thank you for being kind to me, sir. Mr. Parsley was very cruel, though I did nothing against him. Say something nice to me, sir. Please say something more. Will you have a piece of this cake, sir? Please answer me!"

Well then, tee-hee, I'm glad the kettle spurts all over you. It serves you right for being so rude and not speaking when you're spoken to. Didn't they teach you manners?

How still it stands there in the water, that little yacht! I wish a breeze would blow. I wish I were in a sailing-ship, sailing to Africa with Mamma beside me on the deck.

Now go it, Dr. Ford; let fly at him! Now knock the fat pig to pieces. Oh, do! Make his nose bleed! Twist his arms, sir! Please box his ears as you boxed mine.

Why wouldn't you do it? Why wouldn't you knock him down and then take me away with you. I'd be your servant. I'd be glad to carry your guns and boxing-gloves. I'd be your squire and carry your lance, mounted on my palfrey behind your charger. "I'm strong, Dr. Ford. I could follow you to the top of the highest mountain."

Why won't you! Oh, why won't you!

Go on, fat pig, get out! Go away, fat pig, and never come back any more! Nobody wants you. Everybody hates you. We shall all be glad to see the last of you. Go away!

And no one's afraid of your boo!

Now who will be the next to leave, after the girl and the pig
What would I do if they all left together, every one of them,
to leave me alone here. "... alone here." Who said it? How
can an echo say what I never said? "... never said." I'm
so terribly afraid, Mamma. "... so terribly afraid of
Mamma." No, I didn't say that. "... say that." Oh, then I
must be asleep. Yes, I've fallen asleep and all this room has
been a nightmare. "... all a nightmare, all a nightmare, all
a nightmare, little boy. Eh! Oh! Ah! ... forgive my groans,
but I'm not well, as you see. Now if it's a nightmare it's I
that can help you to wake from it. This lady is your mother,
Billy. Won't you look at her more closely?"

"My mother's dead."

"They never quite die, my boy."

There she smiles at me again, smiles all her hate at me.
Oh, no, no, no! My mother was my lover, and she died when
snow was on the lawn. Wicked old clergyman! Wicked old
ogre, you can't deceive me! How silly, to think that I
wouldn't know my own dear mother, who walked with me
through the tall bracken, often stooping to kiss my head.

"Mamma!" She nods without a word.

"Mamma." She lifts her finger where the red ring shines,
as it shone in the garden on New Year's Night. Then it is
her. Yes, it is her. "They told me that you'd gone away,
Mamma; and then they promised me that you were dead.
'She's dead,' said Harold. 'They'll bury her under a stone
and worms will eat her to a skeleton.' He promised that I'd
never, no, not if I live to five hundred, never see you again.
Oh, why have you come back to leave me alone at the top
of the house, and to hate me!"

What dirty little face is this? What bony cheeks and
dripping nose? What crying eyes are those? It's William.
Yes, it's poor little Billy's face, crying in the landing cupboard.

"Now you see that she's your mother, Billy, and that your
mother was never the lady you dreamt about. Best leave

her, Billy. Best run away with me. Shall I tell you where
we'll run to? To a garden, watered by five rivers, and all
the rivers full of fish. On one side the seashore ends our
garden, and on another tall trees for climbing. Peaches and
figs grow against a wall there, and the little boys build
houses in the trees. You'll eat crumpets and shortbread and
ices and shrimps; scrambled eggs and chickens, trifle and
jelly and pies. You'll learn to swim there, Billy. You'll learn
to box and to fence. In my yacht you can go out fishing, to
catch cod and conger, whiting, plaice and dogfish. You'll
stay up to midnight, never say prayers, and sing as loud as
you choose. There are no mothers in our garden, Billy, to
make us cry; no witches, no ogres. There are kingfishers and
humming-birds, gulls on the shore and pigeons in the tree-
tops, but bats are chased over the garden wall on sight. So
come, Billy, come! Come away, Billy, come to the garden!"

_F6_   ***Miss Black***   Those snowy teeth, as false as her hair! Now I'm bound to wonder whether I was wise to come, for there's something . . . oh, INTRACTABLY base in the atmosphere of this room. Well, but intractability was always a fiery spur to the saints, and I must fight here with all the strength He has given me.

"What's your name, little boy? Goodness, child, don't be shy. I'm not going to eat you." (But it's hard to believe that there's a soul here to be saved, anima naturaliter christiana! Yet I DO believe: Lord, help Thou my belief.) "Won't you take another piece of cake. That's the way! And won't you say 'thank you.' And won't you tell me your name. Now do speak up, child!"

"My name's William."

"That's better, William."

Though there's little cause to boast of it. Now there's a face I know, a silly face, a ninny's face, full of silly love. But, for my own fault, I owe attention to such misguided and self-righteous girls.

"I think I USED to see you at St. Aloysius."

"Yes, I used to go there before the changes."

"So you disapproved of what you call 'the changes'."

"I loved love better than doctrine, Miss Black."

"A very delightful sentiment, Miss Tillett. And you trusted your own unlimited wisdom for the proper employment of your love! What do you take to be the function of God's delegates on earth if not to teach us how our love should be directed?"

"We know it by prayer. If our hearts are opened to God, Love is as clear as the sun and the stars."

"Profana simplicitas! Hasn't it occurred to you, child, that the devil can imitate the voice of God? More evil comes from your 'goodness' than from the hearts of wicked men."

"Miss Black, I know that the devil speaks as you do now."

Dear God, indeed I can do no more, and she'll take her wanton error to the grave with her. Love! Why the devil   92 talks of nothing else. Love of this poor moon-eyed girl for her explorer: love of the benevolent for humanity: mother's love and brother's love and love of a moth for a star. Love of God means nothing when the word is so corrupted; for are we to love Him as the shopgirl loves a postman or the sow her farrow! I know well enough that the love of God is constant pain and affliction, and I think, I hope, that those who suffer most here are those who love Him most.

How dare you address me so, you loud-mouthed cockney clown! Now this, of course, is the penalty for appearing in such company, that they can treat me as they treat each other. ". . . I leave the punishment to you."

"I'm much obliged, sir, for your abstinence and kindness."

But no, nothing could pierce that rhinoceros hide. Yet I'd far rather punish the informant than the poor child, and I wouldn't be indulgent if I had THAT to do.

F7   It isn't strange that the boy should hate me, and I must remember that it·was a great hater of the Church who became its finest servant.

"I'll tell you why you don't like me, William. It's because I'm the only person here who cares what happens to you. Do you understand that, William? The others only care that you shouldn't annoy them, but I care about YOU, about the way you treat this life which God gave you. Did you know, William, that you were given a soul, and that your soul can be saved or lost for ever? Won't you come to see me sometimes, and I'll tell you what God wants you to do? You'll come, won't you, William?"

"But I was going to live with HIM, with Mr. Parsley. He told me about his· house by the sea where nobody could hurt me. . . ."

Yes, yes, poor child, the old Terrestrial Paradise, Satan's dream kingdom. The House by the Sea, the Garden, the Kingdom of God on Earth! Who knows as I do the impious charms of the dream; or who knows as I do the bitter shock of waking! In a wicked dream at Tunis I waited, eyes daylong on the sea horizon, and all my heart one sweet, foul dream of love. All a summer Lieutenant Mario Rufini was my GOD. Yes, a worthless boy in blue and braid was the Transcendent and the Immanent; and when he sailed away for ever, then the whole blank world was godless for a year. And then on the shore I built a pyre, seared, by God's grace, with the horror of my blasphemy. And burning on my pyre, I knew that all one hemisphere of the round world is fire, the other, ice. I knew that there is nothing here for us but extremities of pain, to be endured for Adam's sin and ours.

And now, dear Lord, grant that this child may know the wild glories of our pain, the icebound peace of our acceptance, the fire of our renunciation. Make me a vessel for the service of Thy Grace.

"I most sincerely regret, Miss Black, that my intervention in regard to Billy was so unwelcome to you. The more so since I am assured that we are at one in faith."

94

Now it's not, no it's not without advantage to listen to the devil's gibber. Poor creature, he comes here in such an obvious guise, hoof, horn and all, that I'm tempted to laugh in his livid face. Indeed, I suspect that this is some quite junior and inexperienced emissary, for Satan himself would never stoop to obscenity and gross abuse.

"You neither amuse, nor even shock me."

And yet the unrestrained vulgarity of hell does sicken me indeed. I mustn't tremble now, or show my nausea. Be still! Be still! Oh, God, be fiercely tranquil in my heart!

"Let's go thumbscrew each other, Baby."

Yes, Christ my King, drive out the demon from this mortal frame, and leave the wrack to be purged for Your habitation. Now scourge them all with the scorpions of Your Love, for this room is a ripe hell for your harrowing.

There's the Scarlet Woman, spawning all her horrid off-spring around the table. Sharp-eyed Materialism, flushed with anthropocentric arrogance. Doubt with trembling lips and sudden eyes; the poor ugly imp of Fear, and . . . God in His Mercy, can it be a priest of the Holy Church!

"Forgive me, Father. I'd have asked your blessing sooner, if I hadn't been so greatly preoccupied. Teach me, father, to share your peace of mind, for my heart is filled with anger."

"With anger, my child?"

"But surely there are diabolical agencies around us?"

"Around us and inside us, Miss Black, above us and below."

"But in this room, father, preternatural forces?"

"My mistress, though it's the last thing you'd expect at her age, wets her mattress nightly."

"Father, I'm out of my mind!"

"No, no, dear lady. A ventriloquial prank of Charley's with that dog of yours. Now you were speaking of preternatural forces. Then you do sense something numinous about us here?"

"Numinous! I feel it to be diabolic."

"Indeed, diabolic too. The room's electrically charged, and an electric current, I believe, has its negative as well as its positive element. Now I am assured, Miss Black, that your anger is truly of divine origin, and I counsel you to strike at your enemies with all your power, as Our Lord did in the Temple."

"The girl was an enemy of our Church, father—a proud and self-willed creature. With God's help it was I who drove her out."

"A fine achievement in its way, my daughter. But it's Dr. Ford I'd be expecting you to single out. There's a headstrong and godless fellow for you, but a brave man, and determined. It may be that he's not so far from us as he imagines. At least he's aware of man's lowly stature, and he even has a benighted conception of something higher—or in our words, nearer to God."

"I've been a blind and foolish woman, father."

"Now I'd recommend that you deal softly with the man when your opportunity comes. We've learned that the frontal assault, while it ministers to our pride, seldom gives the best results."

"Oh, father, let me strike openly at the devil, with open defiance. I'm quite unskilled in subterfuge."

"Then I fear you must learn it, Miss Black. The mind is no less God's weapon than the heart."

Must I be devious and subtle now, I who have prayed for the joy of open martyrdom? Oh, yes, it is God's will that this last fence of my pride should be broken down. How much more he asks than virtue, than beauty, than truth! Once I believed, as she does now, that the innocent and open heart was quite enough. But the world is misshapen now.

Ah, there he goes, the poor possessed. Humbly I thank Thee for his exile, my Christ, my jealous Lord.

This, then, this lean, impenitent fanatic, this modern Dio-cletian, is my arch-adversary here. And he's a worthy one, I grant, who'd be a Loyola if I could turn him. And I SHALL turn him, and he SHALL know the nightlong horrors of the moon, and all that biting of the moonlit dust in the desert. He'll cry out at the slow amputation of his human heart, and then cry louder at the slow gestation of his godliness. Sanctity will break from him in a travail far worse than any childbirth.

Mario, old drunkard, rotting to an unholy end on the wharves of Genoa, as full of sin as age, now you are quite alone to die, too twisted in vice for any sacrament. Die and burn! Die and burn! Dear God, but Father Morton's sick! For my sin? Because I wished him damned, my old lost lover? Oh, doubtless he's an admiral now, living in a Roman palace.

"Miss Black, is there nothing we can do for Father Morton?"

Nothing YOU can do, you pitiful doubter. It was you who always saw the "good" in everything, and followed it in nothing. Every camp has known the timid incursion of your foot, and learned to despise it. Whoever saw you with a sword or plough in the hand? Why, I remember now how you would run from the sessions of that congress on Intel-lectual Brotherhood to be thrashed by a prostitute for your horrid pleasure. This is our modern practitioner of public benevolence and private shame, damned at birth and court-ing damnation all his life long. "I think I never saw such cowardice in any eyes before." Leave me!

An Office for Extraordinary Grace. Grant, dear Lord, that through this humble vessel of Thy Grace Thy Servant Domi-nic may be cured of his grievous bodily ills. Give him new strength to fight Thy battles in this heretic island of the North. Grant that the soul of the child, William, may be bent to Thy Service, and that this fierce enemy of Thy Church may become her fierce defender.

Now what psalm of saints and angels is in the air about
me? That's the sweet Gregorian of supernal voices.

"Kyrie Eleison"
"Christe Eleison"
"Kyrie Eleison"

Now all is promised in this miracle of divine music. The child shall be mine, and I shall turn the imperious purpose of Dr. Ford to the service of dear Mater Ecclesia. The holy wounds of Father Dominic shall be healed by the Holy Spirit.

Rise! Yes, rise, Dr. Ford, in the last wild fury of your pagan soul. Now it's Lucifer himself who strides about the room, whirling his gigantic arms like the dead sails of a windmill. Christ, I thank Thee that there is no fear in my heart. No, not though he strike me to the ground, as now he does, and though his laughter roll in my ears. Strike again, Dr. Ford, strike again! See how I lift my head to receive your blows. Strike again!

"But ah, no, William, stay!"

F10   "You'll not be forgetting your duty, Miss Black."

"No, father, never. Dr. Ford, you mustn't think that I resent your assault. In fact I'm truly glad that it gives me a chance to talk to you." (So William's lost to me. Then HERE be with me, Lord!) "I know something of your philosophy, and although in many ways it's utterly opposed to mine, I would like to say that I truly respect you as an adversary. I think we both despise cowardice, and have very little use for doubts and hesitations. In fact I think we both know what a low and contemptible creature is modern man. Left to himself what does he ever do but burrow back into the slime he sprang from!"

"Whereas you would prefer him to kneel to a god of his own contemptible invention, a god who shares every one of his qualities, except, Miss Black, the saving one of existence. I have no respect either for you or for your faith, and I cannot conceive that further conversation will be of the least profit to either of us."

He'll pull down the moon from the sky and bury it; pull Christ from his Cross and all the saints from the cathedral walls. Now creatures of a mad perpetual light will build his godless city, agile corpses exherting their doctored limbs on a new Babel, a new Sodom. This is the day of Anti-Christ and a disciplined Pandemonium. His signs, long, long ago proclaimed, were these very miracles of ungodly achievement, the land reclaimed, and mighty impermanent cities built.

Now already I can hear the loud dead din of their camp-fire songs, down in the valley of the National Park. Now I rise to You, Lord of the Ice. Oh, take me! Now all my broken soul is rising to the peace of death. Forty long years of this! Oh, take me, Christ of the Passion, to Your savage breast, and let me lie for ever in the holy comfort of Your thorns.

What hard grey face is this, beneath the serpent hair? What dull charred eyes? What planted crow's feet, wrinkles   *100* and corruscations of pain? Sweet reason tells me that this can be nobody but Janet Black. Then it's no wonder that they never saw the glories hidden by these washed-out features. (And yet this face, this waste of a face, shone once like a jewel on the coast of Africa.) Take me, God my Devastator, and let me hide the devastation of Your love from all this mocking, foolish world. Oh, no, no, I never regretted, never. . . . No, I'd change nothing on this face, except to scar it still more deeply with the blessed wounds of service.

Ha, my poor Doubter, and has YOUR time come? See him fasten his lips like leeches on the gross hand of Mrs. Goodman! How all his doubts and errors festoon him now, and weigh him down! Go away, you sad thing, you broken precursor of the intolerable dawn. Go! Go! Yes, summon what impious dignity you can for your departure, since dignity can't long survive the situation which awaits you. Go away! Go!

F11   Now, father, this shall be my last service here, to show them
how we take our leave. For me there'll be no drama of a
burning, no last proud shout of praise; but dignity at least,
disdain at least. Now bless me, father, as I kneel to kiss
your ring. Reverently, I kneel, and humbly, but not with
ostentation. (Now his holy wounds are foul, with a saint's
corruption.)

  "Father, bless me before I leave."

  "Father Morton, who was the young man called Tillett?"
Oh, couldn't he grant me this at least, to leave in peace!
"Bless you, bless you for your question, dear boy."
Why, why is there such confusion at the end, such shouting and laughter and a band playing, a band on a pier?
Now I know nothing except that I stayed too long and that
God's ways are stranger than ever we predict. (For the
truth is that I'd imagined the end so differently: a hard bed
but a quiet one, and the sacrament from fingers thin as
tapers; the vesper plainsong from some near chapel of the
woods, and a moonlit cruifix on the wall—there on the wall,
there before me.) He's fallen! "Oh, he's dead! The father's
dead! They've killed the father, killed the Church, killed
Truth, killed God!" Now walls and walls around me, door-
less, windowless. Where, where's a door or window? An
empty room, a godless room. "Let me go! You murderous
two—you parricides! Let me go, you, there, harlot, in the
triumph of God's death. Oh, Lady, I beg you to let me go!"

F11

G1   ***Noel Tillett***   Age and death clung about me like the dry flakes of a chrysalis. I danced, and the stinking shards tumbled on the floor around my dancing feet. I danced, and my wings unfolded like flames behind me. I took my mother by the hand: she rose in my arms and we danced the Butterfly, the Morning and the Sun. Juvescence again of year and eye.

Then, at their cue, the brothers entered, wearing the old masks, dancing the same proclamatory steps; this one saying, "I come only to fail"; that one saying, "I come only to triumph." Max took the chair, and fell. Tom took the chair, and it held him. But I (for these dancers are no more than the shadow of a shadow in my dreams) I can see the ignorant hopes and fears behind their faces. I can see the Past and the Future singing on their shoulders. And I have wondered again at their unbiddable ignorance, watching them dance the old steps, yet confident that all's spontaneous, all's extempore, that now they might do this, now that. Max took the chair and stared up astonished from the wreck. Tom smiled in silly pride to find it hold him. Max seeks maternal blessing, yet dances back into the savage tomb of his birth. Tom dreams that he may bid the blue woman a kind adieu; yet he dances the wooden, martial gestures of the dragon-killer, must tear the womb and kill the dragon at the water. What can I do but laugh, as I watch them. Alas, my poor servants!

Max, poor servant, who seeks his babyhood in the antique glories of the south, dancing backwards to the everlasting oblivion of Time reversed, passing from thirty, to twenty-two, to ten, to nothing. Tom, poor servant, who plans the conquest of the barren north, and must achieve it. That one bound to fail, seeing so much: this one bound to succeed so blindly. "Why?" asks Max, and hears a thousand answers. "Who is Tillett?" asks Tom, and hears the one true answer which he shall never understand. He's the blind agent of life renewed ("For what?" asks Max), of the circle's end

married again to its beginning. ("For what?" asks Max, and **G1**
who shall answer.)

So Max must knock on all the forgotten doors of the far
past, and see them open on a blank of daylight. He must in-
quire of every book and dancer, receiving no answer, or
too many, or the brief visionary light of It! It! It! (What was
it? Ah, but I had it. Ah, where is it now?)

So Tom must make his mighty superfluous resolutions,
prepare for grave ordeals, be alert for the treachery of
enemies long, long ago defeated.

Poor dears; poor dolls, why it's even with a doll-like
ingenuity that they take their biscuits, Max moved by the
grace of the hare, Tom eager for the blind resolution of the
bull. But when I take the lamb, I am the Lamb, I am the
Sacrifice. Max Hare! Tom Bull! Poor totem repetitions!

Then Daisy enters to the cue of love, and love glows dangerously about her. She turns on tiptoe for our admiration, then sinks on the chair like falling spray, her head bowed to the mother. *Here comes my bonny bride,* thinks Tom, for, as the bulb predicts the flower, so Tom, blind as the bulb to earth, sky, sun and wind, yet grows in foreknowledge of his single task. While Max, dreaming to his girl of the golden legs, sees gold, sees legs, but still sees nothing of his defeated future.

But the Maiden of the Resurrection dances with a delicate primeval understanding. Taking my insubstantial hand, she makes it flesh by her need of a brother's hand. Whispering in my ear, she brings a sigh of death to my dancing lips. And when she looks at me in love and fear, then I must dance the caves of death into my eyes. But though this prescient love must kill me, yet without its wild behaviour—here to kill, and there to save; here to burn forests and there to freeze an ocean—without this pitiless action of love, the dance would die.

From her dream of the Autumn, where I lay dying and rosy in her arms, Tom awakes me with a military salute. "Tillett, I feel sure I've seen you before." And so you will again, my brave redeemer. You'll ask the same question, receive the same reply, brood and retreat and ponder and heavily advance again. What am I, doctor? Am I your guide across the mountains? Am I the respected builder, and master of the waters? Or am I the dangerous young coward who wooed you to death? Oh no, you must dance your questions all around me, ringed in a spiral leading to that last simple demand: "Who's Tillett?" Then death: then life: then love: then death.

Heavily Max postures, inclines before Daisy, holds out a lean white hand. She takes it. Gravely she dances with him, building, weaving, spinning up his hopes of winning her until he's high enough to die of falling. Now he'll show her his tray of little wisdoms and beauties, as a child shows

its toys. This one he found ten years ago in the forgotten
library of a great house. Here's a cunning fragment of intro-
spection, fetched from the dark diamond mines within
him. Here's sympathy to varnish all his jewels and make
them sparkle with a friendly light. "Take them," he says,
"take all of them, for nobody could wear them so prettily as
you." But Love has a more appraising eye than any poor
collector's. Could she see among these trinkets the ONE
luminous treasure of life, Pearl of Egypt or Golden Grail of
the West. . . . But with the falling twilight Max's jewels
lose all their little glories, twinkle and go out like candle
flames. All's dull and dark about him now, with a smell of
death in the night-time.

Now we're at the midday of the solstice, but still they
dance the unsuspecting steps of childhood. The mother's
still adorable, and the sun still shines. All's well. All's well.
All's well. All's death, at the tiny splash of china.

G3 Within their heads the mother makes her surprising trans-
formation, to harlot here and there to wolf and there to
tears. (For she is nothing but our fear and need.) Each,
in his corner of the darkening room, dances his inward steps
alone. Winter surprised them, falling from the clear sky of
their youth. Night and disgust surprised them. Grief surprised them like an unpredicted storm.

Then see where I rise for my farewell steps, spring once
into the air in petulant regret, fall like a dying bird about
the room. "A God, you blind people! See me dance the
Dying God." Yes, I dance the old news that nothing stays,
not grief, or joy, not dissolution or creation, and the end
of the dance is its beginning. I make little impression. In
their dismay they've no time for wonder or reflection. Some
may regret me, but none will understand what's lost in my
departure. And yet always, at this point, I feel that my part
should have been longer. Is it not exquisite how I take the
broken cup, fallen on one trembling knee, and how I sob,
sob, sob my passage to the wings?

Father Morton At the end of this interminable
passage, a door swings open on the winter, and there hangs
my flippant youth, splayed on the dead oak of the door.
Sweating and stumbling I can—yes—reach the pendant body
—then—groaning—we are one again. Carnivorous age de-
vours the innocent past. "Come, Charley, my Caliban!" And
thus we reel and totter to our winter kingdom.

Hero and Man, Maid and the Mother of Snows, here's
your humble and obedient servant come again at your bidding. For, "When I am young" cries the Old King, "when I
am happy, then I laugh at the ignorance of man, and boast
of my divine omniscience. But I am old," cries the Old King
in his penitence, "and in my age I know that man's ignorance is more wonderful than my omniscience. When I am
young, man is no more than the shadow of a shadow in my

dreams. But I am old, and I am no more than a suffering **G3**
shadow in the dreams of men."

My entry is inelegant (for in their misfortunes they lose
the taste for elegance); hardly a dance now, hardly more
than a mime of age, disease and pain. Such is my obedience
to their winter creed: such an old slave am I! Tom demands
a wilderness of pain to cross and conquer. His brother
craves it to dull his birthday shame, and Daisy for the exer-
cise of love.

Therefore I'm inclined (in these early moments of my
winter return) to doubt the value of my superior knowledge. I know all that each of the other dancers knows or
will know. I am the composite knowledge, past, present and
future, of the human dancers; but nothing beyond them,
nothing outside them, no, nothing from the sky. Soon their
present and their future will be their past. To me it is
their past already. Unlike the arrogant and theocentric
dances of my youth, I am now degraded to mere exposition,
to the tidying up of other narratives, to the filling in of a
few gaps. I am a coda and a belated chorus.

G4 No, in this old age I am no longer intoxicated by my Godhead. Divine knowledge still leaves me far from the terrible reality which man possesses by his ignorance and his imagined freedom.

And for my active role here—distinct, I mean, from this mere setting in order of the over-furnished room,—it differs from man's only in being SOLELY determinate, without even the precious illusion of choice. I am the Death where Life begins. I am the Doubt, the Sin, the Obstacle, to be resolved, to be atoned, to be surmounted. I am the Storm and the Yawn, the Iceberg and the Chilblain, the Tabu to be broken and the Denial to be denied.

Now, for example, I despatch my son on his incendiary mission. He'll fail. It's known already that he failed. Therefore in my youth I would have found the alertness of Tom Ford superfluous and grotesque. But now, an old man and a far humbler native of his mind, I am conscious of his freedom to be too late, or too cowardly, or too clumsy. And, watching his behaviour, I am no less fearful than the others for its outcome.

Now that he has indeed survived the first test of his manhood, the backward judgment of man will be as confident as the forward judgment of a green young god. "His birth and early life ensured that when the moment came he would . . ." Ensured! It's there that they forgot their own uncertainty and terror at the moment when live coals glowed across the hearth.

Daisy's immediate desertion of Max and adherence to the doctor is graceful: it's simple, and above all, it's PROPER. Standing as much outside them as my enslaved condition allows, I delight in the pattern which forms here with the lovely precision of configuring crystals. Yes, yes—(I applaud my own creation)—it was right that the dance should continue exactly so. Yet . . . *why do you stare at my Judas brother, my Cain. . . .* Yet in his choking grief and anger, how should poor Max see anything here of order or propriety? And who shall say that the majestic elegance of the whole is more real than the parochial solitude of this single man, truer than the suffering confusion of this single mind?

"*The answer is Man!*" But how should Max guess the answer when he can never formulate the question? Everywhere he sees a threatening question, and doom in a wrong answer.

Daisy was not to escape the avenging demon of her own action. (Whatever they do here sows the seeds of its own undoing.) Charley, deputed to execute all my uglier and more revealing tasks, conscientiously insults and mocks her, in order (for who can tell?) to drive her prematurely from the room. He does it, poor boy, as best he can, but it's denied him to succeed in anything.

"Don't touch her, Charley!"

For I am also the unbreakable law which must be broken, the old prohibition which must be disobeyed. I am the indignant and implacable Father.

G5 *I know that face. Oh, no I don't; I don't; I won't:—and I won't look again to see.* This baby fear comes as a conqueror and engulfs me. I am become nothing but an ague and a scream in the night, a child's terror of the river caves with the black floors of sucking mud.

And yet (freeing myself from the devouring mind) what is this newcomer but a quite subsidiary performer, one who serves our purpose once or twice, but plays a brief and trivial role? And what is he to the others but, at most, the angry shame of recent birth: at least, a mere indecipherable nuisance?

Billy kicks Max, who shouts and whitens. Billy kicks Tom, who rises with a swirl of his northern dignity, and . . . leaves the room. Yes, our chosen hero is departed, fled from a task which seemed suddenly too arduous and of too questionable a value. Then Daisy lays her head on the table, and pours her golden hair around it. Then Max leans back to laugh. Then Charley claps his hands, and Billy dances a little dance of finality among the teacups on the table.

Oh, no! The foreseen behaviour was observed, and even now I feel the sharp pain in Billy's ears. But dare we say, seeing an alternative so boldly stated, that the other course was IMPOSSIBLE, that man could not die for ever if he wished. (That's my poor Charley's aspiration; but was there ever a creature more impotent against the stars?)

But now his eyes are on the Cross again, on the far hill where his Saviour hung . . . *yet he* . . . *shall feel no warm touch of pride until the castle itself lies before me* . . . *until the old race is extinguished.* In my youth I would have laughed at Daisy's misreading of Tom's exalted gaze. But now I know that these distinctions of faith scarcely deceive them, for I see that Tom, Daisy and the rest believe only in living and dying.

"The good doctor seems very far away from us just now."

So deviously I must address them, for ever concealing my true purpose under a blanket of deceiving words, a meas-

ured flow of lying metaphors! I can never say openly:
"Here's the true nature of your impulse, and this will be the consequence of obeying it." For man has lost the beast's simplicity, and never attained the simplicity of God. So now: "True love," I say, "is love of God and of God's holy order," for I can only lead her to disclose her love by using the terms of her own faith. Were I to say, "You must marry him because the children of your marriage have long ago grown old and died," how, in her temporal subjection, should she understand me? How should she understand if I were to tell her that, by wooing him before his task is accomplished, she must be his enemy before she becomes the proper and inevitable reward? So I must speak to her of duty and of sin. I speak in the metaphor of good and evil, and trap her with her chosen words.

G6 *Those snowy teeth, as false as her hair.* Now I am the dry vagina of old virgins. I am the barren woman's loathing of seed and flower. Yes, now I would castrate and sterilize the world. Now infanticides shall be honoured for each baby delivered up.

And yet (shaken free again, again outside her) I know that her dance, so full of passion and excess, imparts a strange vitality to all who watch or join it. Taking Billy with her long teeth and fingers, she sheds bright colours on his little discoloured body. She hungers to save his soul, and he wriggles to escape her teeth, for teeth and salvation are the same. *"My name is William."* Now the long teeth join over his soul. But this was not until she had stirred him to his brief, brave war-dance of defiance; not until he too had shared in this sad nobility of man, to create a moment's uncertainty where everything is certain. And even eaten, Billy is a eucharist, flesh devoured to give eternal life: even buried, his corpse enriches the eternal soil. How shall he, she or anyone escape it?

Now I'll be as free from them as I can ever be, taking dark shape as the Watcher in the shadow of the hall, in the shadow of the firs (sometimes half-seen at dusk or daybreak). And once again they are no more to me than the changing couples in an old ball. Here the Maiden and the Woman of the Desert have made their old ferocious curtsies and dance the old aggressive steps. One smiles in a bitter longing for triumph: the other shakes a sorrowful, provoking head. And over to the left a wilder couple dances, more violent and dizzy in their paces. Flying from the sting of Janet Black, Billy leaps into the arms of Charley, who hugs him fondly, and then throws him high up to the ceiling. There he stays suspended in a dream of bliss.

Meanwhile I'd slipped from those observant shadows to dance the climax of my old dying majesty. Before Max I dance it, most courteous, most inactive of spectators. Until his exit the quiet passage of his dissolution will hardly break into the melody at all. There's nothing but a dying fall for him, a faint mortal counterpart to the trumpets of his brother's progress. And it was for this that I chose him as the partner for my laborious and artful death-dance.

So now I move in slow traditional periods, showing one face to her, another to him, saying "Do this," to him, "Do that" to her. And all about the feet of Dr. Ford I weave my trip-ropes and hempen nets. I am the spider binding them to action and mortality, and one by one each dying dancer is caught in my false webs of wisdom. "Life is conflict." I dance. "Life is contradiction. There is no resolution. I dance despair. How pitiably narrow is the hero's path, how comically obtuse."

This is the lie of all my dancing—to tell the truth and nothing but the truth, but never the whole truth. To dance Despair without Hope, or Hope without Despair.

G7 In spite of the dignity of my dance it has a dervish quality. Now they begin to hum and buzz about me, stirred to a greater volubility, a wilder action. I've danced the Hero into heroic passion, from stillness into fruitful movement, from silence to his first loud cry of indignation. For now he leaps high up towards the ceiling, his clenched fists thrown above his head, and he shouts the old unbreakable will of man. *"One man arises"* dances the doctor, *"and I am that man."*

I smile with Max: with Charley I belch at the humourless extravagance of Tom's performance. But I know what they forget, that the Hero has always been unsmiling, and that humour is a sly weapon of death. Knowing this, I begin to dance the dry little comic wisdom of death, grimacing and mocking, bowing, shuffling and buffooning. For if I could make him giggle, then, giggling, he'd conclude that life has no great argument to lay against its ending.

And certainly he falters now; the grand, premeditated stream of his eloquence is broken. He blushes, fumbles, searches for a phrase; and should he, at this moment of weakness, look once at my grinning face he'd laugh and be lost. But already he's recovered, and his wooden face shows no tremor of dismayed amusement. No: these little pauses never do more than enrich the will by a renewed apprehension of danger. And Daisy's moment of intervention is badly chosen. Her shy, courageous, futile declaration comes at the very instant of his keenest awareness and firmest resolution. She blushes prettily enough, and all her little arts are used. But already the doctor suspects my disreputable inspiration behind everything he hears or sees. *"Seedy and murderous powers,"* he says, and could he have found better words to describe me?

Yet by this same denunciation he becomes a murderer himself, killing Love for Life's sake. Mist encircles Daisy: sleet falls on her, and everything is washed from her heart except the sudden simple expectancy of death. For Love is the first   *116* victim of Life's reckless persistence. Death and defeat were the seeds which Daisy sowed when she took her love from Max and poured it too profusely on the helmeted head of Tom. The little patient demons of antithesis waited to strike her, struck hard and killed her. And yet. . . . And yet. . . . Yet from her temporary death she'll rise again, the silent fruition of love reborn. From the silence of the passage she'll return again, dead and golden in the morning.

For one who loved so dearly and with so wide a generosity, it's notable how little they'll regret her. I fancy that they sense her curious dispensability. Maidens of simple heart and ardent love—they know there are a million to replace her.

Behind the wraith of Daisy, swaying on the threshold, Charley and Miss Black are locked in a savage embrace. They kiss with the hostile passion of monkeys, conjoin in a mulish infertility. It's only to watch Daisy droop from the room, that they leap apart, stand towzeled, stertorous and bloodshot.

G8 This much I may show them (though too late, for none will understand it until he stands on the threshold)—that Tom's dance is far more murderous than the delicate apathy of Max, far crueller than the gentle path where I would lead them. Dancing my little persuasive steps towards the grave of the world, I proclaim that if ALL would follow then none would suffer. Death is feared by the lonely dier, only because he knows that others survive him, because he knows that in ten seconds, nine seconds, eight, the tall dim figures at the bedside will sigh, relax, and stoop to cross his arms. I urge them that by extinction, instantaneous and universal, they could put an end to death as well as to life and the sufferings of life. But the doctor's wilful progress makes death perpetual. I can make no judgment. I can do no more than offer an alternative to this round of conception, birth and dying, an alternative to be rejected.

"Father, I'm out of my mind."

Yes, to accept the abusive dog so readily shows that. Janet Black is close to the pit (of insanity? of enlightenment?). But in another moment she will be close to the white radiance of the sun (of enlightenment? of insanity?). Everything has been excluded from her senses except the hottest flame, the coldest ice, the blackest pitch; and when, in her leaps from hell to heaven, she sees another who explores the heights between, she's shocked by such unsuperlative behaviour. Man, devil or angel, she labels him an aspiring devil, or a fallen man—for why should an angel descend?

Mighty ambitions and a fat incapacity. I can do no better than take Charley's own self-perception as a text for his obsequies. Death has sprouted in him, and the sweet odour of death hangs about him. My son and servant in this, he has willed death for the whole world—though not as I have softly urged it. No, not with all the veins of the world opened in a lazy sea, incarnadined—but in the loud punishment of fire and brimstone, in the blasphemy of broken bodies.

This was not a man embittered by any particular shame or failure, any more than Daisy was for ever sweetened by some individual act of kindness. Men are so consciously attached to life that they will always discover an "explanation" for suicide or congenital viciousness. But Charley disliked life from the womb. His dislike found golden opportunities for growth, and grew to this catholic impulse to destroy. Thus to himself he became the very principle of destruction. But to others. . . . To others, poor Charley has seldom been anything grander than a naughty clown, whose worst outrages caused only a shocked titter around the teatable.

And whenever he has acted for death he has stung into life, as the malevolent stings of a wasp can save the victim of a sleepy sickness. Indeed, it's the fate of all my dancers to dance the opposite of everything they wished.

"Boo!" he shouts, to his incapacity and fatness.

The stage is emptier, and with each departure my body droops a little lower. Now I've crept into the hidden mind of the child to shine in the self-created darkness of his lie. The dark lie keeps him here, and the light of my revelation will be his death.

Also with each departure the pattern of the dance grows simpler, for the intermediate dancers have obscured the single theme. There's little now but the deceitful conversation of a garrulous old man, and the bombastic progress of a doctor. We two must dance it to the climax, and the anti-climax, while all the others leave, proud in their incomplete divergent visions. This one, on the threshold, sees the everlasting principle of conflict: that one sees harmony under all the martial behaviour: the other sees only fortuitous complexity, misrule and chance.

"They never quite die, my boy."

Yet even he, and even now, though stamped and sealed for early death, lifts up his bloody head like a dying drummer boy and shouts for the life-preserving lie.

Now indeed the dance becomes so simple and so formal that the complexity of my deputed functions is no longer necessary or apt. Their eyes have opened wider and their understanding has crystallized into little certainties of hope or fear. And therefore I can assault the doctor's integrity directly, and in my own person. Openly I can declare myself the Tempter; and it's with all the formal aspects and inflections of the Tempter that I cringe and leer before him, bent on my wounded knee. Recommending the rich food to him, I speak in the honied tones of a dishonest merchant. And it's with the same formality that his incorruptibility displays itself, brusque, contemptuous, seeing me in the colours it had long suspected me to wear.

These sanitary tasks remain—to clear out the remnants of the Dead in Life. Billy was Fear and the Lie, and the little cornered courage of the ignorant. I sing to him of peace, for his only peace is in the final act of death. He has

danced the brief parody of many a more active dancer, **G9**
defying a little, accepting incompletely and dying without
grace. He had no innocence, for innocence comes, not in
childhood but in youth, and never quite vanishes again. Had
he lived longer he might have acquired innocence, and then
the richer guilt of memory and foresight.

Dance, Billy, dance! Leave the air cold behind you with
the terror of the death of children. See where my little
herald of death flies black from the open window. Come
away, come away, life! Such scales have grown about you,
encrusted shards of fear and lies and shame. Dance, Billy!
Max and Janet, dance! Surround this stubborn man with
your falling wings of death; winnow about him the odours
of the grave and urn. No leaves fall in the garden, and the
sun hangs forever at his cool meridian. So come, Billy, come!
Come away, Billy, come to the garden!

G10   "You'll not be forgetting your duty, Miss Black."

A dry injunction, for my mind grows drier as my body liquefies in this premortal corruption. All my eloquence is spent, my virtue exhausted, in this herding of the mortals to their death. My throat's dry, and my bones feel as brittle as kindle wood. Each death brings me nearer to my own, and now my stricken body cries out for the next end and the next beginning, for the passing of the winter solstice and for the awakening in the garden. May it be sweet and soon!

How gladly I'd have Charley with me still, and the whiskied wind of his contempt! What would he say to the seduction of our Unseduceable by this death-struck old woman? How fiercely he'd laugh at the cracks and seams in her dulcet voice, and at the pride of Tom's refusal. For certainly the spectacle of her humiliation is comic, and I can hear ghosts of laughter behind the walls.

He'll pull down the moon from the sky and bury it. So he will—forgetting in his triumph the old moon's resilience. She'll rise again from her tomb, drive women mad again in the forest, touch them again with all sorts of monstrous fertilities. This lady of ice and fire is to survive me, will be my loud but solitary mourner. In her belated departure she'll be a warning against too stubborn a persistence, too brave a refusal to admit defeat. Yet there will be only one survivor to heed her involuntary warning, and he's not the man to discover in her ending any reference to his own condition. So it seems that, for our purposes, Janet Black was no more than an adversary to be defeated, a warning, unintended and unheeded. For the others were blind to the glories of her passion.

Now Max has risen too, to see Death's sudden face above the mantelpiece. The vanquished stand together, but solitary in their separate defeats, the one bewailing her defeated cause, the other glad to die at last. (His dignity was easy to achieve.) So it seems that Max, as he suspected, was no more than a failing contrast to his brother's triumph. For

the others were blind to the treasures which he loved and **G10**
guarded.

At such a stage it may seem a superfluous and pedantic
mockery to press him to mend my walking-stick. But we are
compelled to dance every variation on that theme. An effect
is made by repetition, and perhaps our purpose is really no
more than this—I mean to make an effect. Beat a gong: daz-
zle with a searchlight: repeat, repeat, repeat old words and
phrases. But I grow so tired now that I envy Max the brief
priority of his departure. I grow so tired of the familiar and
the strange, tired of foreknowledge and exhausted by uncertainty. Let them see what they choose, conclude as they
choose, but, heigh-ho, I'm glad that I shall soon be free from
their visions and conclusions. Who began it? Already my
mind is swimming in the clouds of death.

G11 Who began it? Who can end it? My memory falters now, and . . . *Sympathy and Knowledge have been my weapons against the One Man Arises, One Man Arises, One Man arises. Those who suffer most here are those who love Him most, and it's through Love that we surmount ourselves, God's blessed gift. All of you hate me, so I'll hate you back and crumble Cardiff Town Hall on the fat behinds of the Welsh.* Life is . . . Death is. . . . No, my wisdom is exhausted and I have no valediction.

What if he does wake in the garden! He keeps little of this identity, for this identity is only to be old and tired.

"Bless you, bless you for your question, my dear boy!"

Away, dear doctor, with this old ignoble season! Raise the young sun in the sky! The air grows blue about me, pale sky-blue darkening into cobalt, into purple, into the night. I think there was something still to be said, a last word to shine in this night. Gush at the neck now, and all's liquefaction.

Noel Tillett The water sings in the hollow banks, and plays through the whorls of my shells, my ears. Now the dancing water runs across the uncovered pupils of my eyes, sluicing, rinsing, ringing sleep away. There are the hanging faces, through the water, hanging from the branches and the sky. "Come, ladies, take me up! Take up the wet and wounded body: anoint it with the violet and narcissus. Anoint the scar at my neck where once . . ." (But why should I remember!) "Heal with your lips the little wounds at my feet and palms, the tusk-hole in my side." Sweet Gethsemane again: sweet Garden of the waters and the women.

The sun had risen three hours when their task was finished. And then, singing the resurrection songs, they led me through the golden garden to the door of my mother's house. I kissed their open lips, and danced away into the colonnade, easing my limbs from the icebound winter of sleep. In the hall I took the Graal: it shines and increases in my hand, shines in the eyes of my mother as I hold it high above me. Mayn't I take her in my arms at once, to dance the Butterfly?

But long arms are twined about my ankles . . . ugh! An ape-like creature kneels at my feet with bloody eyes burning on the Graal. What if I kicked him backwards, and danced across his sprawling body to my mother's arms? *"I kneel to the detonations of the thawing rivers, the ice-blocks flowing from the ice-bound harbour."* So the eloquent monkey is blasphemous in his ignorance! "Kneel to me, Monkey; kneel to Me and My Graal. There's nothing else to kneel to here."

Well, but there is some ceremony to perform (my mind's still heavy from the lethal waters). The hairy doctor has some claim on our gratitude. (Imagine it!) I must—oh, horrible!—kiss his sweaty forehead, and then, and then. . . .

G12 Yes, set down the graal before the looking-glass, and dance this way, that way, this way, that, scattering the primroses to right and left. For nuptials are to be celebrated here, between the Living and the Dead. Violet and primrose, crocus and daffodil; I scatter them about me as I dance. They fall upright on the floor, grow from the floor in a bright and aromatic carpet.

Prancing and capering, nimble as a breeze from the western sea, I dance to meet the bride. She stands at the garden door, naked in the golden garden, one of those whose faces hung above me from the apple-tree, dancing above me through the dancing water. I take her by the hand and we dance together to the marriage room, dancing the Dove, dancing the Sun and the Ring.

Still the simian warrior kneels there, sweaty in his brazen armour, hot with blood among the flowers. My mother has twined a dark wreath of laurel, and as we enter she leans to him and lays it on his iron crown. Then from the garden comes the paean of the singing women, singing the triumph of the Ape of Life. And I have led the silent girl, the dead and smiling girl, to kneel beside him in the violets. I take a garland of festered lilies, touch them on the radiant Cup so that they light up, so that they unfold into stars of snow. I lay them on the golden head of the bride, and in the garden the women are singing the Marriage of Life and Death. I join the white hand and the hairy paw: fingers twine deep down among the flowers, and the garden is singing the Seed and the Conception.

"Dear friends, by this act I make one flesh the Monster of Life and the Maid Entombed. By him her tomb shall be rich with a curious progeny, alternate children of light and darkness. You will be cursed by shameful tantrums in the nursery, and by savage monkey-faces glaring from the cupboard under the stairs. You will be blessed by happy laughter in the woods, and by children dancing on the shore. And one shall follow in his father's laborious footsteps, trampling   *126* down his father to be started on his quest, fighting with his mother to be free from the tomb of his birth. I see him in the wings already, impatient to be settled with his parents. He stands stiff and expectant in the shadows behind you, his face aglow with the aggravation of his boredom. On his shoulders gleam the brass crowns of his majority. It is he who will lead your city into arrogant war, enslave the neighbouring tribes and found a new empire to decline in syphilis and civil dissension, to fall, in love of death."

"But when I am old," cries the Old King in his penitence, "I know that even in terror and decline there will be moments by starlight, fruit devoured on the seashore after swimming, and a song from across the river. And one child will be spared from the city's ruin, to be cast like bread on the sea."

Now I dance, and my wings unfold like flames behind me. My mother rises in my arms, and we dance the Butterfly, the Morning and the Sun.